"Fascinating," Ms. Morrigan said.

"You're not hungry again today, Lorelei?"

"Not really," I answered, watching the students around me shovel food into their mouths as fast as they could. It was amazing. We hadn't been here a whole week, and it looked like some of them had gained ten pounds.

Were we being fed? *Or fattened up?*

SPLENDID ACADEMY

THE SINISTER SWEETNESS

of

SPLENDID ACADEMY

Nikki Loftin

Illustrated by
Brenna Eernisse

razor
bill

An Imprint of Penguin Group (USA) LLC

A division of Penguin Young Readers Group
Published by the Penguin Group
Penguin Group (USA) LLC
345 Hudson Street
New York, New York 10014

USA / Canada / UK / Ireland / Australia / New Zealand / India / South Africa / China
Penguin.com
A Penguin Random House Company

ISBN: 978-1-59514-628-1

Library of Congress Cataloging-in-Publication Data

Loftin, Nikki.
    The sinister sweetness of Splendid Academy / Nikki Loftin.
        p. cm.
    Summary: In this twist on "Hansel and Gretel," two middle schoolers find themselves in a new charter school filled with a mysterious abundance of food at mealtimes and sinister teachers up to no good.
    ISBN 978-1-59514-628-1
    [1. Middle schools—Fiction. 2. Schools—Fiction. 3. Witches—Fiction. 4. Magic—Fiction.] I. Title.
    PZ7.L8269Si 2012
    [Fic]—dc23

                                2012012167

Printed in the United States of America

1 3 5 7 9 10 8 6 4 2

For Dave,
Cameron,
and Drew

Contents

CHAPTER 1:
Splintered

When my mom was alive, she read me stories every night. "Use your imagination, Lorelei," she'd say, "and your whole life can be a fairy tale." I wanted that to be true. But I should have paid more attention to the fairy tales.

Because not all of the children in them come out alive.

And sometimes there are witches hiding in the woods.

My soon-to-be stepmother was a witch, I was sure of that. I wasn't quite certain whether she wanted me to die, but it was looking possible. Die of humiliation, if nothing else.

Somehow, she had convinced my dad to make me wear a peach-and-white petticoat dress, with white shoes that looked like they'd been stolen off an American Girl doll.

They were about that big, too. I could feel the blisters coming up as I walked to the minivan.

"Hurry up, Lorelei," Dad shouted from the front seat. He already had the engine on. "I don't want to be late for my own wedding. Molly will kill me!"

"Molly's already trying to kill me," I murmured as I shut the door. I hadn't been quiet enough. Dad had heard.

"Lorelei," he warned. "Molly is not trying to kill you. Why do you insist on being so negative about her? She's going to be your new mother—"

A rude noise came from the back seat. Bryan, my older brother, had pulled out his earbuds to listen in. "*Step*mother," he said. "She's not Mom."

Mom. The word hung in the air like sparkles of dust in the sunlight, bringing with it memories and pain. My heart thumped hard against my seat belt. Nobody said anything for a few seconds. Nobody breathed. I closed my eyes so I wouldn't have to see if Bryan was giving me the look he'd given me over a year before.

The day I had destroyed our family.

At last, Dad cleared his throat. "No, Molly's not Mom." I opened my eyes. His face was reflected in the rearview mirror, sadness settling into the lines at the corners of his mouth. "But she's important to me, and we love each other, and she loves you kids. That's why we invited you to take

2

part in the ceremony. I know you'll be the finest flower girl and groomsman a dad could ever ask for."

Bryan pretended to puke.

"Bryan! I expect you both to make some effort. Be nice."

"I'll be as nice to her as she is to me," I heard Bryan mutter.

As nice as Molly? That wasn't asking much. I started to hum the Darth Vader theme from *Star Wars* and when Bryan laughed, I did, too.

Dad frowned. I thought he was mad at me, but he was just disappointed, as usual. He was staring at my hair. "Did you even try to get a brush through that mess?" he asked.

I knew I'd forgotten something. "Sorry," I said. "I'll do it at the church."

He put the van in reverse and sighed. "What happened to my princess?"

I didn't answer. We all knew what had happened.

I looked down at my palm and started picking at a tree-climbing splinter that had gotten stuck in there the day before. The splinter didn't hurt. Not nearly as much as the memory of my mom; that throbbed and tore at me all the time, like a splinter I couldn't budge.

I had been a princess. My life had been perfect. I had been Daddy's best girl, my room stuffed full of Barbies and decorated with a pink bedspread and flowery curtains.

Maybe Molly would have liked me more if I was still that girl: the coloring-book, rainbow-cupcake, dollhouse kind. We could have made friends, like Dad kept begging me to do, over makeup and curling irons.

I looked out the van window, watching a bunch of bull-dozers pushing earth around, changing the shape of the land as fast as they could. A tall woman, with black hair pulled back under a hard hat, walked across the site, pointing things out to the workers with a small branch—probably from a tree I'd climbed. Changing my neighborhood.

I should have been used to it. Everything in my life had changed—permanently.

We passed the Willow Grove city limits sign a few minutes later, and I finally gave up trying to think of a way to make Dad smile again. Sucking up to Molly wouldn't be enough, I knew. Even if she was the nicest stepmother in the world, even if I wished we could be friends, it wouldn't fix what was wrong with our family.

Me.

CHAPTER 2:

Splendid Academy

Three excruciating days later, on the way back from the wedding, the flower girl torture was over and we were all out of nice.

Dad was driving back home, quieter than usual and definitely not smiling, with my new stepmonster, Molly, in the front seat. Bryan was in the back, as usual, his ears stuffed full of headphones.

I was looking out the window, thinking about calling my friend Allison once I got home, when I saw it. It was the construction site I'd noticed on the way to the wedding, the one with the bulldozers. But there were no bulldozers now. Instead, there was a building. A completely finished red brick building with bright yellow doors, sparkling clean windows, and a sign. "What is that?" I murmured.

Dad didn't answer. Bryan did.

"Can't you read, ignoramus? Oh, I forgot. You can't. It's a school." He read the words super slowly, just to be mean. "Splendid Academy: A Charter School for Grades Four to Eight."

"I'm not an ignoramus, you jerk. And I can read fine. I just can't write very well." Bryan had spent the last year either ignoring me or making fun of my kindergarten hand-writing style. My fifth grade teacher had bugged Dad to get me tested to find out exactly what was wrong with me. She said it might be dysgraphia, and she wanted to get it checked out so I could use a computer keyboard for my exams. Maybe even get some help—there were all sorts of therapies, or so she said. But Dad never got around to filling out the testing papers. He had a lot on his mind, he said. I understood. We all had a lot on our minds last year.

So I wasn't sure if I really was dysgraphic or not. Maybe I *was* dumb. I smacked Bryan in the head, anyway, just on principle.

"Cool it, Lorelei!" Dad warned. "Molly has seen plenty of your behavior this weekend. Both of you."

I guessed he was referring to the incident at the hotel

when Molly told the wedding guests she was planning to be "the best mother a child could have." I probably shouldn't have made that gagging sound so loud everyone could hear. But later I'd overheard her privately telling the minister at the reception she thought it was God's will Mom had died, to make a place for Molly in our family.

Really, throwing a glass of ice water on her head hadn't been the most terrible thing I could have done.

Bryan yelling at everyone to get back because "the witch was melting" sure hadn't helped, though.

"Dad! That school. It just . . . appeared!"

"We don't shout in the van," Molly said, not turning around. It sounded like she was gritting her teeth. "It's not polite, sweetheart. And schools don't just appear. It's been under construction for a while, I'm sure."

I hated it when she called me *sweetheart*. That was Mom's word. "Excuse me, Molly," I said, trying not to sound as impatient as I felt. "But they just started building it last Friday. It's brand new. And it's finished."

"What did you say, Lorelei?" Dad asked. He was making googly eyes at Molly, and he didn't look either.

"Remember that site that was just bulldozers three days ago?" I tried again. "I saw it when we were driving out of the neighborhood. Look at it now."

"It's not polite to demand, sweetheart," Molly said, her voice as fake as Velveeta. "You should ask with a 'please.'"

"Dad. Just look at it?" Someone had to look. This was unbelievable. I'd spent a lot of my free time that summer exploring the drainage ditches near my house, the ones that butted up against the lots that were still under construction. So I knew that it took time—a lot of time—to go from bulldozers to bricks. There was all sorts of stuff they did with plumbing, foundations, lumber, drywall, and roofing materials. I wondered for a second if this was a movie set. It couldn't be real, could it? And built in three days?

"Please," I begged, "somebody look."

But Dad had stopped at the stop sign and was staring into Molly's eyes. "You'll make a wonderful mother, darling," he said, as if I couldn't hear him. "You've got the knack."

"I wish. But you know what they say," she whispered back. "Practice makes perfect."

"Mmm, now there's a thought." Dad leaned over to her. "I know something we should practice. Pucker up, gorgeous."

I stuck my fingers in my ears and closed my eyes so I didn't have to see them kiss.

But I opened them as we went around the corner toward our street, and—I couldn't help it—shouted again. "A playground!"

Bryan had obviously turned off his iPod, because he whistled long and low. "Would you look at that!"

It was the most elaborate, most breathtaking playground I had ever seen. It took up what must have been two acres, with every single piece of equipment you could imagine. There were monkey bars, swings, climbing frames, and slides, all brightly painted and gleaming with newness. I even saw some of the old equipment that was practically outlawed at other schools—I counted two carousels, four seesaws, a high bar, and two high balance beams. I wasn't any good at gymnastics, but I'd stolen Bryan's old skateboard at the beginning of the summer just to bug him. He hadn't cared, though, and I hadn't practiced much. But maybe the playground would be open on weekends and I could use one of the balance beams to learn a trick or something.

I wished I could get Bryan to hang out with me again. We never did anything together anymore, not since Mom died. Well, besides fight.

"Check it out," Bryan whispered and pointed to a grove of trees near the edge of the property. They were some kind of tree I hadn't seen before, with silvery leaves. I followed Bryan's finger: Was that a tree house in one of them?

"Wow," I said, "it's got everything." My head buzzed while I stared, humming louder as we moved past. My curiosity

faded, replaced by a strange, burning need to throw open the door and run out to the playground. It almost hurt to stay in the van.

"Is that a chess board?" Bryan asked. Through his window I saw it, a life-sized chessboard with red and black painted pieces as big as me. Just beyond that was a rock-climbing wall that must have been thirty feet tall, and two zip lines that stretched from the edge of a soccer field to a tall platform near a half-sized football field, complete with goalposts.

"That is the coolest playground ever." Bryan's voice was soft, like adults talk in church. I guess he'd forgotten for a minute that he was a teenager now, and he wasn't supposed to get all worked up about kid stuff. But I knew how he felt. It was like looking at a miracle. The playground couldn't have been any more wonderful, even if every kid in the world had voted on what to put in it.

Suddenly, the sun came out from behind a cloud. The light hit the ground around the playground equipment and filled the whole area with a dazzling brightness. It hurt to look straight at it, and I had to cover my eyes.

"What is it?" I asked.

"I don't know," Bryan said, his voice muffled under the buzzing in my mind. "Glass?"

And then the sun went behind another cloud, and I saw.

It was sand. Crystals, actually. The whole playground was covered not with the usual mulch or pea gravel, but with tiny white crystals, each no bigger than a crumb. It was the most beautiful thing I'd ever seen, but for some strange reason, seeing that sand made me want to cry.

"I want to go there," Bryan whispered, still staring at the playground as our van got farther and farther away. "That school looks amazing."

I nodded. I wanted to go there, too. Even if it had appeared in three days, even if it was too good to be true. I didn't care. I pressed my flushed face against the cool glass of my window and wished I could go there.

Wished it with all my heart.

CHAPTER 3:
Dangerous Favorite

My wish came true—in a horrible sort of way. The next evening the whole family (oh, and Molly, too) watched Willow Springs Middle School burn down on the nine o'clock news. Some sort of fault in the wiring, the news guy said. All the students would have to be bused across the district until the school was rebuilt. The only other middle school was on the opposite side of Willow Grove. I had been in it once, for one of Bryan's basketball games. It was old, had graffiti all over the building, and smelled like bleach and cigarette smoke.

Molly had a fit about the distance. Dad muttered for an hour about "substandard test scores" and "educational black holes."

Bryan and I both knew our prayers had been answered.

"Why should we go all that way every day," Bryan asked Dad, "when there's a brand-new school practically right next door?"

"We can't afford private school for two kids," Molly interrupted. Dad had to explain that charter schools were free, just like the regular schools in our district.

"It's not the money," Dad said. "Although I hear those charter schools sometimes have extra programs they *do* charge for."

Molly looked like she wanted to kill the idea if it cost a single cent.

"But think about it," I said, before Molly could speak. "What if we get sick at school, and Molly has to drive across town to pick us up? It's so far."

That stopped her. Molly agreed that would be way too inconvenient, even if she didn't say it quite as bluntly. "They've got a point," she murmured into Dad's ear. "Let me go and check it out. It'll give me a chance to spend some mom-time with the kids."

So Dad sent Molly, Bryan, and me to check out the charter school. A giant banner had gone up out front, reading SPLENDID ACADEMY: A CHARTER SCHOOL FOR GRADES FOUR THROUGH EIGHT, PROMOTING ACADEMIC EXCELLENCE IN A FUN, UNIQUE ENVIRONMENT. OPEN HOUSE 9 A.M.–1 P.M., SATURDAY, AUGUST 13.

Of course, it was already one fifteen. We'd gotten there late thanks to Molly and the hour she had taken to glop on about forty pounds of makeup.

"No one's here," I said. "We've missed it." There were no cars out front, and no parents, kids, or teachers to welcome us. When we got to the front doors, they opened soundlessly.

"Wow! Automatic doors on a school?"

"Well, go on in," Molly fussed. "I thought you kids were in a hurry."

"But there's no one here," I complained. "What, are we supposed to show ourselves around?"

"No, of course not."

The voice surprised me, and I jumped. It was the lady I had seen on the construction site. She wasn't beautiful, exactly. Her black hair was pulled back in a clip, but it fell around her shoulders and shone like a blackbird's wing. Her skin was flawless, even though she didn't have any makeup on. Her nose was a little too long, and her lips a little too thin for her to be a magazine model. But her eyes were amazing. Green and hypnotic. She was tall and . . . striking. Looking at her was like staring at a campfire. I was mesmerized.

"I'm Principal Trapp," she said, and smiled, her teeth glinting almost as white as the tile floors we stood on. "And you must be Lorelei and Bryan." She shook our hands. Normally, I thought it was strange to shake hands with an adult, but shaking hands with her felt right. She looked at me as if we were equals, as if I was someone important.

I smiled at her without even realizing I was doing it, then cleared my throat. "How did you know our names?"

Principal Trapp laughed, and the sound echoed through the empty hall. "Oh, you! I've been hearing about you from all your friends. They say you're a particularly talented singer, isn't that right?"

"I guess I was. I used to take private lessons," I said. "But not anymore."

"Why not?"

Molly interrupted me before I could answer. She was probably afraid I would tell the truth: that we didn't have enough money for private *anything* lessons these days, or so she and Dad claimed. "Lorelei gave it up," Molly lied. "After years! Can you believe? Kids spend all their time goofing off these days, don't they?"

I found that I was so angry I couldn't speak. But the principal could.

"Goofing off? I don't know," she said softly. "I suppose some do. But this one doesn't seem the type. Lorelei, what do you say?"

I started to tell her that my stepmonster was full of it, but

Molly drowned out my voice. "If you had to live with her, you'd see. She takes her brother's old skateboard and runs off all the time, mostly when there are chores to be done. Look! There's not a patch of skin on her knees. It's terrible." She smiled at the principal like *don't you agree?*

The principal smiled back, but when she looked down at me, she rolled her eyes and I could practically hear her laughing at Molly.

A different, soft voice behind me did laugh. "Well, who actually needs all their skin, anyway?"

I whirled around. A woman who couldn't have been more than twenty-five stood there in dark jeans and a bright blue silk blouse, smiling. She had golden blonde hair piled and twisted on top of her head in the most elaborate braids I had ever seen, straight out of a wedding hairstyle magazine. Her eyes were the same bright blue of her shirt, and her teeth were as white as Principal Trapp's. She held out her hand.

"I am Ms. Morrigan." I shook her hand, but let go quickly. It was cold, almost popsicle-temperature. Maybe charter schools kept their air conditioning turned too low.

"I'm Lorelei."

"So you're the girl we've been waiting for." She leaned down and whispered so that only I could hear her. "Very rude, you know. Are you habitually late, or was this a special occasion?"

I stepped back, stunned. I didn't even know her! If this was the sort of teacher they had here, forget it. They could bus me across the district, I didn't care. I almost said it out loud, but those blue eyes flashed again. She straightened and spoke louder. "Lorelei. Lovely. So different. Is it a family name?"

"Not really," I mumbled. I had hated being Lorelei most of my life. Adults always asked about it, like having an unusual name would make me more interesting. They were disappointed when I turned out to be nothing special. For a second, I was tempted to explain anyway—how our normal dad had named Bryan after his uncle, and our fairy-tale obsessed mom had picked mine from an old German legend—but I just shrugged. I wasn't going to tell this woman anything about myself.

"There's a story there, I'm sure," she replied, and turned to my brother. "And you? 'Big Bryan' Robinson? I've been hearing about you, too. I can see where you got the nickname." Bryan puffed his chest out. "I hear you'll be starting on the high school football team in a year or two." Her eyes sparkled. "You are a strong boy, aren't you? Are you sure you're only thirteen?"

He ducked his head and shrugged.

"Not big enough for football yet, though. We'll have to see what we can do about that."

Principal Trapp laughed and put her arm around Ms. Morrigan's shoulders. "Oh, Alva. Lorelei, Bryan, I'll have to warn you: She loves menu planning almost as much as she loves working with kids. If you decide to come to Splendid, and you're not careful, she'll try out a thousand new recipes on you." She shook her head, smiling at the teacher. "Sometimes I worry about how much time you spend in the kitchen. You need to—what's the expression?—get a life!"

Molly must have gotten sick of being ignored. "Principal Trapp? Could we go ahead with our tour of the facilities?"

"Why, of course!" She took Molly's arm and tucked it in hers. There was something old-fashioned about the way she did it. "Alva? Why don't you take a break. We can meet up in the cafeteria later."

"Where else?" Ms. Morrigan asked, and waving goodbye to Bryan—who blushed—she slipped down a side hallway. I jammed my elbow into Bryan's ribs, to let him know I'd seen.

"Pretty," Bryan muttered and shrugged.

"Pretty *weird*," I said. Now that the teacher was gone, the air in the hallway seemed warmer, more inviting.

"Kids?" Molly called back to us, impatient again. Bryan and I hustled to catch up, so we could hear the principal.

"This is the art room, and this is our computer lab. Of course, all of the classrooms have computers for each student as well. We're cutting-edge at Splendid." We turned left and went down another hall. "This is the library. We have over five thousand books, and we have plans for every student to write a book this year as part of their English studies. Those books will all be bound and shelved here for future Splendid students to enjoy."

"No good for you, stupid." Bryan whispered to me, but the principal had heard him. She turned and raised an eyebrow.

"You don't want to be an author?" she asked me, and a little wrinkle appeared between her eyebrows. I wanted to rub it away, restore her face to perfect smoothness. "I can't imagine that."

I was trying to think of what to say, when Bryan broke in. "It's more like she *can't*—"

Molly stepped on his foot with her black high heel. "Now, Bryan. Be kind." She smiled at the principal. "I'm sure she'll learn to love writing. She just needs higher expectations."

The principal looked at me again, waiting, but I didn't say anything about my writing problem. I had overheard my dad tell Molly that he didn't want the school system labeling me a "short bus" kid. He and Molly pretended I was normal. He'd told me more than once that if I practiced more, I would be a better writer. But I worried he really thought I was dumb.

Maybe I was. All I knew was that every year of school got tougher.

When I didn't answer, Principal Trapp started walking again. "Next door is our science wing." I looked at Bryan and he stared back. A whole science *wing*?

"What about music?" Molly asked. "Of course, Lorelei sings."

"I used to, anyway," I said.

"Oh, I wish I could sing!" The principal patted her dark hair back, even though none of it had come loose from the clip. "I'm afraid I couldn't carry a tune in a bucket, as the saying goes. None of my family can, unfortunately. But we've found the perfect music teacher. She's coming from overseas, and I expect her any day. Until then, we'll have an extra recess during music period."

Extra recess? I had never heard of a school like this!

We turned a corner, and Bryan spoke up. "Who are they?" He pointed to six framed photos clustered high on the wall. I stepped up to one. It was a picture of a small red brick school, with a few dozen children standing outside, squinting into the sunlight and smiling as wide as they could.

Bryan read something out loud. "*Escuela de—*" He broke off. "This isn't even English. Where was this?"

I peered at the frame in front of me. Sure enough, there was something written in a foreign language, but I couldn't tell which one. The caption had little marks over the words that didn't look like anything I'd ever seen. One of the students, a dark-haired, skinny girl about my age, stared out of the frame and straight at me. I stepped right up to her, wondering, what was her story? Her eyes were saying something. I felt a gentle touch on my shoulder.

"Those are my students, from the Splendid Academies I've opened all over the world." Principal Trapp waved her hand. "Romania, Austria, Germany, Mexico, Brazil, and Greece. All my former pupils. I remember every single child I've ever brought into my schools." Her eyes shimmered for a second. "They become a part of me."

"That's a lovely sentiment," Molly said, obviously impressed. "I'm sure they feel the same about you."

"I hope they do," the principal said, taking Molly by the arm. "Now, shall we?"

They took a few steps, but I was still looking at the dark-haired girl. "What was her name?"

"Whose?" The principal sounded startled.

I wondered if she really could remember each one of those kids, or if she had just been lying to make herself sound better. I pointed to the girl and said, "This one."

Principal Trapp's lips curved up in a gentle smile. "That one. Of course. One of my brightest. Her name was Vasalisa."

"Weird name," Bryan said.

I stepped away from the wall. The eyes of the girl followed me down the hallway, though, like she was still trying to tell me something. *There you go again with your wild imagination, Lorelei*, I thought, remembering the words my dad had said to me a thousand times. *Focus.*

Molly was chattering away to the principal about test scores when we passed the only door that didn't have a label next to it.

"Principal Trapp?" I asked. "What's this room? Can we go in?"

"Oh, that?" She waved a hand at it and turned away. "Just the teacher's workroom. Nothing interesting."

But I was curious. "I've always wanted to see what was inside a teacher's workroom. They never let us go in at Russell Elementary."

Principal Trapp smiled, but she seemed distracted; Molly was walking on ahead. "Fine. Just a peek; it's not finished yet."

She held the door open a crack.

"Oh," I said, disappointed. There was nothing in there, just a couple of chairs and—weird. "Is that a table?" I asked.

In the corner, leaning up against the wall, was a giant dome-shaped . . . something. It was covered with a black cloth with strange markings embroidered all over it along the sides. It couldn't be a table, though. Wrong shape. And

one edge near the bottom was uncovered, just enough that I could see a gleam of copper.

Maybe it was a drum, a kettledrum. Did this school have a band?

"Principal Trapp?" I looked back, but she had already gone down the hall with Bryan and Molly. I ran to catch up.

"And this is the heart of our school, the most beautiful room—in my estimation—in the building."

She opened the door, and Bryan and Molly gasped. So did I when I caught up.

"The cafeteria," Principal Trapp said, and smiled.

We stepped in.

I'd never seen such an amazing cafeteria. It was only a medium-sized room, but it looked more like a restaurant.

Small tables, covered with bright tablecloths and center-pieces made from peacock tail feathers and glittering glass balls, filled the room. Rich velvety purple fabric hung like enormous pillows from the ceiling, and giant crystal and gold chandeliers floated over each grouping of table and chairs. The chairs themselves were works of art, carved wood and gold leaf, straight out of a fairy tale. The arms of every chair ended in tiny gargoyles' heads, with each gargoyle making a different funny face.

"Sweet!" Bryan started running toward the table in the center of the room, the one with the fountain centerpiece sculpted into what looked like chocolate mermaids. "Got anything I can eat?"

"Bryan, don't run inside," Molly warned, but the principal touched her arm lightly, and Molly stopped.

"Yes?"

"It's perfectly fine. He's just excited. We want the kids to be excited about their food. They'll be eating at least two meals a day in here, and we tried to make it a second home."

"This is nothing like home," I said. "This is amazing." I ignored Molly's dirty look.

"I'm glad you approve. Ms. Morrigan is responsible for the design. She even oversees the cafeteria staff. I tell her frequently that she works too hard. She's been planning the school menus for months!"

Months? How hard could it be to come up with hamburgers, pizza, and chicken nuggets?

"I mostly pack my lunch," I said. "It's safer than our old school's cafeteria food."

"I can imagine! They practically starved you all, I hear." She sighed, and I smelled peppermint. "No wonder you're so small. But haven't you eaten this summer?" She took one of my arms between her fingers, and squeezed a tiny bit. It made me shiver all over, in a good way, the way I used to when my mom brushed my hair. "Don't you eat at home?"

Molly laughed, and pulled my arm back. "That's just Lorelei. She's so active, for a girl. And she's got her mother's metabolism."

Molly sucked her own stomach in. She wasn't skinny like my mom had been, and I thought it bothered her. I had heard her and Dad arguing the night before about why Molly needed a five-hundred-dollar-a-month personal trainer at the gym when they didn't have enough money to pay the cable bill. She had yelled something about needing to slim down so she could measure up.

I wanted to tell her that she would never measure up to my mom, but I didn't. I *can* be polite.

Molly frowned. "Did you say they would eat here two times a day?"

Principal Trapp nodded. "Yes, breakfast and lunch."

Molly tilted her head. I could tell she was thinking about how much extra that was going to cost. "Oh, I don't think the kids will need to eat breakfast at school. We have plenty of time to feed them in the mornings, since we live so close."

The principal bit her lip. "Oh, but breakfast is the most important meal of the day. The staff at Splendid has found that when the children eat here, under supervision, they have a more productive day. And the kids love the food. Pancakes, bacon, omelets, French toast. And it's all part of our Community Schools grant, so it's free of charge."

"Free of charge?" Molly looked interested for a moment, but then shook her head. "Well, I'm sure Bryan will love that, but little Lorelei won't touch a thing. She won't even eat dry cereal most mornings."

"Is that so?" The principal knelt back down by me. She touched a finger to the top of my head, and pulled a piece of hair loose from my ponytail. "What beautiful hair you have, Lorelei. Spun gold. Is it naturally curly?"

I nodded, the lovely goosebump feeling back again.

"I thought so. I knew a little girl a very long time ago with hair just that color, hair that curled exactly as yours does."

Her voice sounded sad, and I wanted to comfort her. Was she talking about someone who had died? Maybe she had had a daughter, one who looked like me. I didn't say the words out loud, but I saw her nod anyway. Then she straightened up, smiling.

"Well, you may rest assured that you will love our food. We hire only the best chefs, and use the freshest ingredients. What do you like to eat?"

I wondered what I was supposed to say. I knew there was always a right answer with adults, and they never wanted to hear the truth. "Broccoli?"

Principal Trapp laughed like I'd made a joke. "Lorelei! No, really, what do you most love to eat? If you could have any food in the world, anything at all, as much of it as you could hold—more than your parents would ever let you have—what would it be?"

She waited for me to answer, like what I might say mattered to her. Before I could, though, Ms. Morrigan appeared at the doorway behind us. She had papers in one hand. "Principal Trapp?"

"Yes, Alva?"

"You have a call. Should I take a message? Or I could finish the tour for you."

"Oh, would you? I was just asking Lorelei what her favorite food is. Maybe you could have the staff make it—that is, if we're lucky enough to have this very special girl and her brother join our school." She leaned down next to me, and looked me in the eyes. Her eyes were green, dark and deep as a forest, pools of green that I could fall into and float on, forever. "Do you want to join us at Splendid, Lorelei?"

"Yes."

Her eyes brightened. "Good. Good." She patted my arm and straightened up. "I can't wait. Thank you, Alva." In a flurry of apologies to Molly and Ms. Morrigan, the principal left.

"So. Your favorite food?" Ms. Morrigan's voice was as cold as her hand had been, and her lips twisted up into a pinched smile.

I didn't want to answer, but I made myself be polite. "Marzipan."

"Marzipan?" Her laugh made the crystal chandelier tinkle overhead.

"What's funny?" I asked, confused. Marzipan wasn't that weird.

"A dangerous favorite. Maybe you are a special girl. Why marzipan? It's an uncommon sweet here in America."

I shrugged defensively. "I just . . . it's good."

Molly broke in. "It was her mother's favorite. Her mother is German, or was German, I mean. From Germany German, not just German American." Molly started blabbering on about how my mom had died suddenly the year before, but Ms. Morrigan was ignoring her, I could tell, even if she seemed to be listening.

Molly went on until Ms. Morrigan handed her some paperwork to fill out. Then the teacher led Bryan and me outside. "That's where everyone else is."

"Everyone else?" Bryan asked.

"Why, of course." She had that hard smile again. "You didn't think you were the only students, did you? Just the two of you? There wouldn't be enough to go around!"

Enough to go around? I wondered what she meant, but then she opened the doors. Bryan yelled—"The playground!"—and disappeared.

The sounds of dozens of kids playing on the world's best playground filtered through the doors, and my feet itched to go out and join them—but I stopped. I had to ask one more question.

"Ms. Morrigan?" I called out. She was leaving the cafeteria, but she turned back.

"Yes?"

"Why is marzipan a dangerous favorite?"

Her gemstone eyes glittered.

"Marzipan is made from almonds, Lorelei. As is cyanide, one of the most fatal poisons. In ancient times, those chefs who prepared marzipan frequently died from it. Even here in America, some people will crush bitter almonds in water to try to cure themselves of terminal diseases. It invariably kills them faster than the illness."

I swallowed hard. I'd never seen anyone look like she did when she was talking about poison. Like she was remembering a particularly lovely dream. I tried to joke about it.

"Marzipan . . . can kill you? I'd better not eat any more then. I love that stuff. I'll probably die within a month."

"Die within a month? Ridiculous. You're far too small to die." She frowned, then brightened, her face smooth and beautiful again. "Of course, that's not a topic for children. Go on out and play. I think I see your friend—the little Grey girl."

I looked, and it was Allison. I hadn't seen her in weeks, maybe months. Not since she'd spent the night at my house, and we'd talked about what had happened to Mom.

Allison waved, and I forgot about the creepy Ms. Morrigan, the marzipan, and the fact that we had all just agreed to go to a new school with all new teachers. I was happy for once. Allison was there, and she was waving at me, and everything was going to go right for the first time in years. I just knew it.

We played for hours, until the sunset turned the sand pink and gold, and Dad drove back over to pick us up and take us home.

Chapter 4:

The First Day of School

The first day of school was foggy and cooler than usual. We could barely see the front doors of the school through the fog; if it weren't for the sign, we might have driven right past. It was strange crossing the parking lot, holding Dad's hand like a little kid.

For some reason, I remembered that morning when we went to see Mom in the hospital together. He had held my hand then, too. He had held it all the way to her room, where I had seen her lying there, hooked up to tubes and machines, casts on both legs, and I had known something horrible was going to happen.

All of a sudden, I felt a surge of fear.

"Dad, I don't want to go," I said, and yanked on his hand.

"What? Don't be ridiculous. Molly said you loved this school! You and Bryan both begged to be signed up." He patted me on the head like I was a dog. "You're just feeling nervous. There's nothing to worry about. Bryan will help you if you need anything. Right, Bryan?"

Bryan didn't answer until Dad reached over and pulled the earbuds out.

"Yeah, sure. I'll watch out for her." Bryan looked at me. "They know she can't write?"

Dad frowned at Bryan, and I mouthed the words "I'll kill you" behind Dad's back. Bryan just rolled his eyes.

"That's enough of that, young man. You two are sister and brother. Family. Family takes care of one another, right?"

Dad waited. We didn't say anything. As far as I was concerned, Bryan could take care of himself, and I sure wasn't expecting him to help me in any way. After Mom died, he had turned into a typical brother, from what I could tell: a stranger I had to share a bathroom with.

"Right?" Dad waited for us both to say "right" before we crossed the lot.

Dad walked us up to the door, where Principal Trapp waited. She looked even happier than she had two days before.

"Mr. Robinson! It's lovely to meet the father of these

two bright children," she said. They shook hands and Dad smiled.

"You must be Principal Trapp. It's good to meet you, too. I was just going to walk the children in to class—"

The principal took hold of his arm, and he stopped talking. Her long fingernails rested lightly on his shirt-sleeve. "I'll have to ask if you can leave them here with me. We want to help our students learn to be independent, and we have found that when parents walk their children to class, it undermines the students' growing sense of responsibility."

"Well . . ." Dad looked torn. He glanced back and forth from me to Bryan. "Lorelei was a little nervous, this being her first day."

"*Daaad!*" I couldn't believe he was ratting me out.

Principal Trapp put her hand on my shoulder and squeezed. "She'll be fine, Mr. Robinson. I'll take her to her classroom personally."

Great. The whole school would see her walking me down the hall like a kindergartener. Lucky me.

"Well, okay, then." Dad hesitated, then kissed me on top of the head and ruffled Bryan's hair. I smiled; Bryan hated that. "I'll see you kids after school. You're walking home, right? It's just a few blocks."

We nodded and said goodbye. Dad had only taken

a few steps away when the principal's voice cut through the fog.

"Mr. Robinson?" she called softly. "It really would be best if the children could come at seven thirty tomorrow, as I discussed with Molly. The whole school breakfasts together. It's a sort of . . . team-building time."

"Oh! Well, I usually eat breakfast with the kids. It's our time together, since I work late most nights." The principal raised one eyebrow, and I swear my dad blushed. "Is it really necessary?"

"Yes, it is. I'm sure you understand."

Dad shifted his weight back and forth. "I know you spoke to Molly, but I was hoping we could find a way around it. It's kind of a tradition in our house. Breakfast with Dad."

"Oh, dear," the principal said. "I'm so sorry. I'm afraid it's one of our requirements. The teachers eat then, too. It's a very important time of the day, and your children will have a wonderful meal. Maybe you can start a new tradition? Dessert with Dad?"

"Sure," Dad said. He turned abruptly and walked away, not glancing back.

"I'll make sure you get something special for snack today," the principal was telling Bryan when I turned back around. "You can't learn on an empty stomach."

Bryan thanked her and jogged off toward his classroom.
She turned to me, and her smile was warmer than sunlight.

"You, too, Lorelei. You'll want to catch up with your
brother. Oh, dear!" She glanced up at a clock that hung over
the door. "Time to catch up indeed. It's later than I thought.
You'll miss the whole morning if we move this slowly." She
grabbed my hand. "Let's run."

Run in the halls? I couldn't believe it. She *was* a real
principal, wasn't she?

The question must have shown on my face, because she
laughed and answered. "I'm the principal, Lorelei, so I get

to make the rules. And the first rule is, do what the principal says. If the principal says run, run!"

We took off together, laughing, practically flying over the tiles. I was breathless but happy when we got to the doorway to the sixth-grade homeroom. Principal Trapp wished me luck, waved goodbye, and walked around the corner.

I felt my head to make sure my ponytail wasn't too messed up and looked at the class list hanging outside the door. There were only fourteen names, all marked present except for mine: seven boys and seven girls.

I scanned the list for girls I knew: just one, but it was the one that mattered. Allison Grey, my best friend since third grade. Well, maybe not so "best" for the past year. But I felt like we could really be best friends again, here at Splendid Academy.

Allison hugged me when I came into the classroom. "Oh, my gosh, Lorelei. You're never going to believe this. Check out our desks!"

She pulled me over to her desk, which was carved like the chairs in the cafeteria. It was old-fashioned, with the chair and the table part connected. Every desk was decorated in gleaming jewel colors, and the name of each student was painted in large, looping cursive letters. Mine, which was next to Allison's, had been written on with gold ink. I'd always liked the way my name looked in cursive, but this was the best handwriting I'd ever seen. The giant *L* was gorgeous; it looked like a swan swimming toward the edge of the desk.

"Amazing," I agreed. Allison's name was written in fuchsia, her favorite color. I looked around. The other kids were all working already.

Well, I suppose *working* wasn't exactly the right word. Two of the boys had handfuls of M&M's, and they were throwing them at each other's mouths, missing half the time. Three of the other girls were curled up on beanbags on a giant tapestry rug, texting on their phones. To each other, probably. They were giggling quietly and drinking what looked like fancy cappuccino slushies.

I stared at the tapestry rug. It was beautiful, too. I was beginning to think nothing in this school was plain. The design on the rug was strange, though, with a large tree in the center, and some kind of animal half-hidden behind it. I couldn't quite make it out, so I craned my neck around to see.

A voice I recognized stopped me.

"It's a very famous tapestry design, one of a series called the *Hunt of the Unicorn*. This one is titled *The Unicorn Tries to Escape.*"

My stomach turned as I realized the animal behind the tree was a unicorn being speared by dozens of men on horseback.

"Lovely, isn't it?"

Lovely? I looked up. Ms. Morrigan stood there, wearing a sunshine-yellow dress. Oh, great. She had to turn out to be my teacher, didn't she? I remembered her cold skin and, hoping she wouldn't shake my hand or anything, took a step back.

"Whatever you say, ma'am."

The room filled with laughter like silver bells chiming.

"Oh, Lorelei, please! You make me feel so old. I want you to think of me as a friend. So no more *ma'am*-ing. Promise?"

"Yes, ma'am. I mean. Yes. I mean, okay, miss."

Everyone started laughing then. Allison laughed, too, harder than I had ever seen. It made me feel weird. Jealous and angry.

"Yes, Ms. Morrigan." I lifted one of my eyebrows, and finished softly. "Ma'am."

"Have it your way, dear," she said, and something in her blue eyes flashed, like lightning far away. "It's time for our first lesson, anyway."

She moved off, and I noticed that the air where she had stood felt cold and smelled strange. It was a familiar scent, but I couldn't put my finger on where I'd come across it before.

I sniffed again and knew. I had only smelled it once. Lilies. At my mother's funeral, the neighbors had sent an enormous arrangement of lilies, tall white flowers that smelled so sweet, I had almost gotten sick from them at the service.

Wonderful, I thought. *My teacher's perfume smells like death lilies.* This was going to be a long year.

"Isn't she beautiful?" Allison whispered as she sat down. "And super nice. She sat next to me at breakfast. Why'd you miss? They had this whole welcome assembly thing. And the food was amazing."

I was about to ask what she'd had when she pulled out a permanent marker and started drawing something on the side of her desk.

"Allison? Stop! What if she sees you?" Allison was more of a goody-goody than I was.

"It's fine, Lorelei," she said, and gave me a look. I knew the look: Bryan gave it to me all the time, a look that plainly said I was stupid. I had just never seen it from Allison.

"Ms. Morrigan said we could do whatever we wanted to with our desks. They're ours. This isn't Russell Elementary." Her eyes were shining brighter than Ms. Morrigan's. "They treat us like adults here. We can leave the class whenever we need to go to the bathroom, and we don't have to raise our hands. We can eat or drink anything we want in class, and talk on our phones or text as long as we don't distract the other kids. Kendra asked about report cards, and Ms. Morrigan said we even give ourselves our own grades."

"What?" I whispered. "That's nuts! No school in the world works that way."

A hand landed on my shoulder.

"Splendid does, Lorelei." It was Ms. Morrigan. She smiled down at me, but my shoulder hurt where she gripped it. "If you had come to breakfast you would have learned what a very special school this is. Different from any other kind of school in the world. Better."

"Better than Russell?" I mumbled. "Sure."

Ms. Morrigan leaned even closer, and whispered in my ear. "Poor thing. If you had another school nearby to go to, I would send you this very morning. Too bad someone left their ovens on and burned every last desk and chair. We'll be more careful here."

"Ovens on?"

Willow Springs Middle School had burned down because of a wiring problem, hadn't it? And the school kitchen didn't even get used in the summer. Why would my teacher say it had been ovens?

I was about to ask, when Ms. Morrigan put a finger to her lips and made a shushing sound. "Our little secret, hmm?" Smiling, she let go of my shoulder and moved away.

My stomach churned. Was it because I was completely creeped out, or because I was getting sick? I couldn't tell.

I peeked over at Allison. She was popping M&M's into her mouth.

"Can I have one?" I tried to smile. I didn't want Allison mad at me.

"Fine," she said, shrugging. "But you have your own. They're in your desk."

I looked, and sure enough, there they were. A shallow, golden bowl filled with candies.

"Candy in our desks? Why?"

I was just wondering out loud, but Allison answered. "Candy math, Ms. Morrigan says. We eat as much as we want, and we'll do math problems with what's left."

I looked up. Sure enough, on the chalkboard it said CANDY MATH: 10:30. Right after MORNING RECESS/SNACK TIME. Wait—there were two snack times written down.

"Crazy," I whispered. Two snack times, plus breakfast and lunch? "We're all going to be fat."

Come to think of it, I was sort of hungry. I hadn't eaten very much at breakfast. Too nervous. I reached into my desk and pulled out my bowl of candy.

I tapped the edge of the bowl. It was real metal. For a second, I had a wild thought. Was it real gold? But then I shook my head. No school had that much money. I emptied the M&M's out and laid them on the letters that spelled my name. I had enough to cover every letter, with one red one left over. I was about to pop it into my mouth, when I felt a hand on my arm, stopping me.

"Don't eat it."

A boy was holding my wrist. A really, really fat boy, who had scooched his whole desk toward me. I thought I recognized him from the grocery store, or the park, or somewhere, but I'd never talked to him; the suburbs are a big place. He had dark black hair that stuck up in cowlicks all over his head, chocolate-brown eyes, and a red Smithsonian Museum T-shirt that stretched tightly across his stomach.

I glanced at his desk: His name was Andrew. Was he trying to steal my candy? Bryan did that all the time. I gave him a nasty glare. "What, you want it? Get your own."

But he wasn't looking at me; he was staring at Ms. Morrigan's back. "I have my own."

"Then let go." He was really starting to tick me off. And my arm hurt.

"No, seriously. Don't eat it."

"Why not?"

He peered down at my desk. "Lorelei? That's your name?" He whispered so softly I almost couldn't hear him.

I nodded. Ms. Morrigan was moving down the row, setting textbooks out on the desks she passed.

"Pay attention, Lorelei. What do you notice?"

I twisted around in my chair. The classroom was quiet. Everyone was busy.

Then I noticed the sound. Chewing. A dozen mouths chewing, cracking the outsides off handful after handful of M&M's. Some students were reading or writing. Some were texting or playing games on their phones. But every one of them was eating as fast as they could.

"So?" I said, not wanting to admit I found the sight of them all shoveling candy in as fast as they could kind of disturbing. "What's your deal?"

He breathed the words; I had to strain to hear.

"They can't stop eating."

"Huh? You're nuts."

He shook his head; if anything, it made even more cowlicks appear, as though he had just rolled out of bed.

"I mean it. You don't believe me? Check out your bowl."

I did, just to get him off my case, and froze.

I knew I had emptied my bowl of candy out. But now, it was full. I examined my desk again. Yes, there they were, the candies lined up over my letters, gleaming red, yellow, green, blue, and deep brown on the wooden surface. And there, in my bowl, sat another large handful of M&M's. Waiting, shining in the morning light that poured in the large windows behind me. Maybe I had two bowls in my desk? I bent low to see. No.

"What are you searching for, Lorelei?" Ms. Morrigan's voice startled me. I glanced up too quickly and hit the bridge of my nose on the edge of the desk.

"Um, a pencil," I lied. "The lead broke off mine."

She walked over to her desk to get me a newly sharpened one.

"Here you are." She laid the pencil and a reader down in front of me. "We're beginning on page forty-two. A retelling of an old Russian fairy tale about Baba Yaga. Read it, and then write your own, with a different ending. Can you do that?"

She moved on, and I looked back at Andrew. He was pretending to read. His fingers kept twitching toward his desk drawer, though. Like he wanted to reach for the M&M's.

"Andrew?" I whispered. He just shook his head.

"I'll tell you at recess," he mouthed a few minutes later. "But don't eat anything before then."

CHAPTER 5:

A Terrible Joke

At recess, I waited for Andrew on the swings. Allison was eating snacks with a bunch of the other girls. It smelled wonderful—freshly popped popcorn covered with caramel, candied peanuts, and giant pitchers of soda. I was starving, but I had watched all the other kids eat what had to be two pounds of M&M's apiece that morning, and I knew something was wrong.

Andrew came over to me, holding two bags of popcorn.

"Here, hold this," he said. "Pretend to eat, so the teacher doesn't bug us."

"Bug us?" I asked, then stopped. Come to think of it, Ms. Morrigan had asked me a dozen times if I didn't feel well that morning. She kept noticing I wasn't eating any of the candy. I finally lied and told her I was lactose-intolerant. She hadn't known what to say to that, I guess. She'd called the cafeteria on her classroom phone, though.

"So, why was it so important I not eat any candy?" I asked, reaching into my bag of popcorn and rummaging around in the kernels. The smell was heavenly, so I stuck my head in the bag to sniff.

"It's addictive," Andrew answered, tossing a few kernels from his bag onto the ground, where they gleamed caramel-golden on the white sand.

I stopped rummaging. "Addictive? Seriously? How do you know?"

"Didn't you notice?" He smiled a little. "I have a problem with food."

I tried not to look at his stomach, where the T-shirt was wrapped around his middle like a sausage casing. I didn't know what to say. One of the big rules at any school is that you don't make fun of other people, at least not to their faces. But I had to say something.

"Okay, I can sort of see that," I said at last. "But what does that have to do with, you know . . . the rest of us?"

He smiled wider. It was a nice smile, even if his two front teeth were a little crooked. "I went to a lot of counseling this summer. You may not know it, but I've lost forty pounds already."

"Whoa," I said. Now I really didn't know what to say. That was a lot on a kid his age. "Good for you," I managed.

"Thanks. The thing is," he went on, tossing a few more kernels over his shoulder, "I learned about trigger foods at counseling. M&M's are one of mine. When I start to eat them, I can't stop. And not just candy, then—I'll eat anything. It actually hurts if I don't."

"It hurts if you don't eat?"

"Yep. I have to stuff myself to make it stop. And even then, it's . . ." His voice trailed off. "Quick, pretend to eat something."

I did, without looking where he was looking. I knew it had to be the teacher watching us. I kicked the ground at my feet, sending up showers of white sand that sparkled brighter than anything I'd ever seen, billions of miniature diamonds. For a minute, the beauty of the sand distracted me, but then I remembered what Andrew had said.

"So, trigger foods?"

"Yeah," he said. "Look at all the other kids."

I did. They were stuffing their faces, eating even while they played on the equipment. "They seem really . . . hungry."

"They're not," Andrew whispered. "Or they shouldn't be." He scuffed his own foot in the sand. "We all had breakfast this morning. So much breakfast. It was the same as this dream I used to have, with piles of sausages and pancakes, syrup, butter . . ." He rubbed his stomach and groaned a little.

"Are you sick?"

"No," he said. "Just hungry. Hungrier than I've ever been in my life, actually."

He looked straight at me, and the world suddenly narrowed all around us, so all I could see were his eyes. "I know how to live with hunger. I've read a bunch about the science of it, studies on insulin resistance and glycemic loads. They taught me in nutrition counseling how to make better choices. How to say no to things like white bread, candy, sodas." His eyes grew fierce. "I have to eat. But I can control what goes in my mouth now. At least, I could for months . . . until this morning."

"What happened at breakfast?"

His voice broke a little. "It was like it used to be. I ate one bite of egg. Protein, right? It should have been safe. But one little bite, and my stomach started hurting. Burning. It was my trigger feeling, even though eggs aren't a trigger food for me. So I stopped eating. And I saw the other kids."

"What was happening to them?"

"Nothing you would notice," he said with a sad smile. "Unless you had food issues, like me. How many eggs do you think a normal kid can eat at once? How many pancakes?"

"Not a lot. Maybe four eggs. Five pancakes?" I ventured.

"Well, that one over there?" He pointed to one of the girls who Allison had been hanging out with all day. *Instead of me*, I thought. "What's her name?"

"Kendra," I answered. "I think." Not that she'd talked to me.

"Yeah, that's right," Andrew said. "Kendra. She ate at least eight pieces of French toast. And the short blonde girl, Mackenzie? She ate like a linebacker—at least twenty sausages."

"No way!" I choked on a laugh. He had to be pulling my leg. Andrew nodded toward Allison. "I was sitting next to your friend at breakfast. Allison, right? She ate fourteen pancakes, seven eggs, nine pieces of bacon, and three whole waffles. Oh, and four cups of hot chocolate. I counted."

"No," I breathed. "That's impossible." I'd slept over at Allison's a dozen times, even if it had been a year now, and I knew she almost never ate breakfast. She said it made her stomach hurt if she had more than a piece of toast. "You're kidding, right? Punking me?" I looked around for the camera. Could be a camera phone, I thought. Maybe someone was taping it all, trying to see if I'd fall for it.

"Wrong," he said. "I thought it was impossible, too. She's so small. But she ate like she'd never seen food before."

"Give it up, Andrew. Joke's over." I laughed, waiting for

him to admit he was making it up. But he didn't say anything—just sat there, looking like I'd said something to hurt his feelings.

"I wish I was joking." He shook his head slowly. "I thought maybe you would see it, too. Maybe we could tell your parents about it. You and your brother are the only kids who weren't there at breakfast. I thought, if I could keep you from eating the candy, you would be able to see what I was talking about." He whispered so softly I strained to hear. "There's something wrong here, Lorelei. Very wrong."

If this was a joke—and it had to be—it was starting to get old.

"Now you're just getting irritating, Andrew." I stood up. "Joke time's over. I don't know why you were jerking me around anyway, but I'm going to tell Ms. Morrigan if you keep it up."

I looked into my popcorn bag, but I wasn't hungry anymore. I was too annoyed. I twisted the top of the bag shut and walked across the playground toward Allison and the other girls in our class. The white sand around their feet was littered with dozens of wadded-up popcorn bags. Two of the girls—Mackenzie and Tess, I remembered—were rubbing their stomachs like you do when you have a stomachache, but no one stopped eating popcorn, not even for a minute. Allison smiled up at me.

"Isn't this the best popcorn you've ever tasted?" She stuffed another handful in her mouth.

I shrugged, and looked back at Andrew. He was swinging by himself, throwing popcorn over his shoulder one kernel at a time.

Allison was waiting for an answer. "Yeah," I said, and untwisted the top of my bag. "It's the best. How many bags have you had?"

She rolled her eyes. "I don't know. Two? Who cares? It's so good." Mackenzie and Tess had their mouths full, but nodded enthusiastically.

Watching Allison stuff her face, I wondered if, just maybe, she *had* chowed down like Andrew said at breakfast. No, he couldn't have been telling the truth. But something was up. My stomach felt upset anyway, so—just to be on the safe side—I didn't eat my popcorn. But lunch was only an hour away, and I had to eat sometime.

Chapter 6:

Bon Appétit

Lunchtime came too soon.

Each cafeteria table had seven students sitting at it, except mine. We had Ms. Morrigan in our group plus us seven kids, all sixth graders. I didn't see any other teachers in the cafeteria. It must have been her day to do lunch duty.

We were seated by college-aged waiters wearing black trousers and white shirts who took our drink orders and went to get our food for us, just like in a fancy restaurant. They were really good at their jobs, and fast, even though none of them talked. I thought it was sort of freaky, but I didn't say anything about it.

I didn't say anything at all. Ms. Morrigan kept staring at me, like she was waiting for me to do or say something wrong. I could feel her eyes on me all the time. Did she know I was thinking about her? I tried not to look her way, but my eyes kept sliding over.

"Where's the food?" I heard one of the girls at the next table whisper. No one answered, since just then Principal Trapp walked through the door and clapped her hands three times for our attention.

"Students? Thank you for listening." She spoke low, soft enough that we all had to get quieter to hear her. I smiled; my mom had used that trick on me and Bryan a thousand times to get us to pipe down. A pain shot through my stomach. Hunger, maybe. Or maybe just the normal pain of thinking about Mom.

"I hope you have been enjoying your first day at your new school. In fact, I want you to think of this as your home away from home." Her eyes twinkled as a boy yelled, "Nicer than my house. Can I move in?"

"I'm not sure we have any beds at the moment," she said over the laughter that followed. "But I'm flattered you asked. I would like you all to remember what I told you this morning at our breakfast assembly." Her eyes settled on me, and I ducked my head down, suddenly shy. I had missed the assembly, of course. "When I started the first Splendid Academy many years ago, I chose the name for one reason, and one reason alone. Splendid Academy isn't called that because of the teachers or the principal. It isn't named for the food or the furniture. There is only one thing that makes Splendid splendid."

Another voice rang out. "The playground?"

Principal Trapp's laughter pealed out so loud the chandeliers overhead tinkled with her. "Some of you might think so. But no. The word *Splendid* refers to you. Our brilliant, magnificent, shining students. The children that fill our halls with laughter and our rooms with learning. Students from all across the globe have learned to shine at Splendid Academy. I'm so pleased that now it is your turn to share your spark with us. Here's to a new school year, and a new Splendid Academy!"

The whole cafeteria burst into applause and cheering. Silverware rattled on the tables as some of the boys pounded their feet.

Principal Trapp glowed with happiness. I stared at her, wondering when I had felt that happy. Had I ever? As she walked out of the cafeteria, my feet tapped the floor, like my legs had voted to go with her.

"She's something, isn't she?" Ms. Morrigan was still glaring at me. My feet stopped moving. "What do you think, Lorelei?"

"About the principal?" I swallowed. "I think she's . . ." I

stopped. There wasn't a word that fit Principal Trapp. "Splendid," I finished weakly.

"Yes, she is," Ms. Morrigan said. "Splendid." The way she said *splendid* made it sound like a bad word. Like she was cursing at me.

Then the food arrived, and I forgot what I was thinking about.

I don't know how they had done it, but they'd cooked every single thing that was on the favorite foods lists I had been making since kindergarten. Pasta with rich tomato sauce, fried chicken that smelled the same as my grandma's, mashed potatoes, carrot coins swimming in honey sauce, and white rolls so fluffy they reminded me of clouds.

"*Bon appétit*," Ms. Morrigan said.

"Huh?" One of the boys at our table looked confused. "We're going to learn foreign languages, too?"

She shook her head, reached over, and handed him his fork. "Dig in," she instructed, and we did.

From the first bite, I was caught in a dream. Each bite was better than any school food, of course. The pasta sauce was rich and spicy, the fried chicken crispy and golden. But as I ate and ate, scooping the sweet carrots up, stuffing the pillowy rolls into my mouth in two bites, I realized that this food was better than any restaurant I'd ever eaten in. Heck, it was better than anything even my mom had cooked.

The thought crashed into my brain like a boulder into a pond. Better than Mom's? Nothing was better than her food.

Nothing in the world.

The fog lifted from my brain, and I looked down. There were seven chicken leg bones on my plate, and crumbs everywhere, all over the red satin tablecloth. Half-eaten carrot coins spilling like crescent moons between the table settings. No one in the cafeteria was talking. No, the only sounds were chewing, swallowing, crunching, and occasionally, a mumbled "More!" or "Yum!" And then footsteps as the waiters came out again, bringing more food, and still more.

I was the only kid not eating.

"Aren't you hungry, Lorelei?" Ms. Morrigan looked at me strangely.

I put a hand on my bulging stomach and realized that, yes—even after I had eaten all that food—I was still hungry. In fact, I was starving. I felt like I hadn't eaten a bite for days. I would *die* if I didn't get some more food. I snatched up a half-eaten carrot coin and put it in my mouth. Ms. Morrigan nodded, said, "Good," and turned away to look at the boy on her right.

"You're not eating enough, Zachary," she said.

I might have kept eating if I hadn't seen Ms. Morrigan do what she did next.

She reached out, pushed Zachary's sleeve up his arm, and encircled his bicep with her hand. She frowned. Zachary was really skinny, even though he was eating more than anyone else at the table. Ms. Morrigan grabbed the butter dish from the center of the table and moved the entire stick of butter from the serving dish to his plate.

And then, in three bites, he ate the butter, the whole stick, plain.

"Yum," he mumbled. "More."

Ms. Morrigan snapped her fingers and a waiter scurried over, placing another stick of butter on the serving dish and a new one on Zachary's plate.

I gazed down at my own plate, at my fork piled high with mashed potatoes, and felt sick. I set my fork down and placed my napkin on the table next to my plate. "I'm not hungry," I said to myself. I whispered it a little louder, since my stomach was rumbling, accusing me of lying. "I'm not hungry."

"Not hungry?" Ms. Morrigan's voice was harsh, a raven's croak. I looked up. She cleared her throat. "Lorelei? You say you're not . . . hungry?"

"No," I lied, trying to keep my fingers from twitching toward the fork. "I'm full."

"Full." She said the word like she had never heard it before. "Full," she repeated, wrinkles forming between her eyebrows, her lips tightening. My stomach cramped, hard. The room grew colder. I fiddled with the tablecloth, then glanced up quickly. For an instant, I caught a flash of—I don't know. It seemed crazy, but her face looked wrinkled and old, like an apple left out in the sun, covered with black, pitted spots and scraped red across the cheeks and nose.

I blinked, and when I opened my eyes, she was staring at me, beautiful again. I rubbed my hand over my face, wondering if I was really sick. I was imagining things—that was for sure.

"What seems to be the problem, Alva?"

I almost jumped out of my chair, and then realized who it was. Principal Trapp was standing right behind me. I let out the breath I hadn't realized I'd been holding. *Thank goodness.*

"The girl says she's full," Ms. Morrigan replied, face turned downward like she was afraid to look at her own boss. I peeked at the principal's expression. She looked interested, maybe a little concerned.

"Full already? You haven't even had dessert."

She kneeled down and gazed into my eyes. I didn't want to look away; her eyes were greener than grass, deep and thick, green as vines climbing castle walls, green as moss in a forgotten forest.

They were the same green as my mother's.

I thought of my mother for a moment, trying to ignore the stabbing pain that came with the memory. Tears prickled behind my nose. I sniffed, trying to hold them back, but one tear spilled down my cheek. Principal Trapp caught it on a napkin and wiped my face gently.

"Oh, Lorelei," she said after a minute. "You are full, aren't you? Full of sadness." I could tell she wanted to hug me, but she didn't. She probably thought I would be embarrassed.

I closed my eyes for a second, and wished the principal and I were alone. Wished I could tell her why I had been so sad for so long.

My Mom left me, I would tell her. *She . . . died. She fell.*

Of course I didn't say anything out loud. I never talked about Mom. I couldn't tell the principal about it. I didn't want anyone to know what I'd done.

My secret. My shame.

I felt a scream building up inside, a scream that would tear me apart when it came out.

She died and left me alone. No one to love me, if they knew my secret. Of course, no one in the world could love me now. Could they?

After they learned I killed her.

I opened my eyes, my heart pounding like I'd won a race. The principal was standing up, staring at me curiously.

"Lorelei? You closed your eyes for a minute there. Are you tired?" She shook her finger at Ms. Morrigan, pretending to scold her. "Alva, you're working the kids too hard. Remember, you have all year. Don't exhaust them in the first week." She paused. "And take care of yourself, too. You're too pale. Make sure you eat something."

"I'm just tired," Ms. Morrigan said.

Tired, I thought. I was tired, too. I blinked, my eyes thick and heavy. I felt like I'd fallen asleep. Had I? How embarrassing!

Ms. Morrigan's shoulders shook, as if she were holding back laughter. Like she knew a secret joke. Was everyone in on it? I took in the tables around me. The waiters had cleared the plates, and the kids were talking to each other. No one else had noticed me nodding off in the middle of lunch. Or so I hoped.

Principal Trapp smiled at Ms. Morrigan. "They're all full, I think. Time for class. Not for naps." She shook her finger at me this time.

"Principal Trapp?" I asked, uncertain. "Did I say something about my . . . ?" But she was already walking through the doors. Ms. Morrigan clapped her hands for the wait staff, and in minutes every plate was cleared.

We all went back to class, in noisy groups—we were allowed to talk as much as we wanted in the hallways at Splendid. No one else seemed to notice anything strange had happened at lunch or said anything at all about the food, except to complain that they wished the teacher had let them eat another helping. Nobody seemed to notice how much they'd already had.

Except for this: In class, after our second official snack time (taffy, which I rubbed spit on and stuck to the underside of my desk, even though my stomach was roaring for more), three of the kids had to unbutton their jeans to breathe.

I would tell Dad about the food that night, I decided. See what he thought.

CHAPTER 7:
Forgetting

When I got home, I knew there was something I was supposed to do, something I wanted to tell Dad, but I couldn't remember what. I had the same feeling at my last voice recital, when I'd stood up to sing and completely forgotten the words to the song I'd practiced for six months.

My mind spun in circles all afternoon. I could remember my classes and playing on the playground. But there was something else, something that hadn't been right. Something Dad would help me with. My head hurt when I tried to think about it, though, and it was time for dinner. So I washed up and decided to stop trying. I could figure it out tomorrow.

"How was school?" Molly ladled mashed potatoes and

carrots onto my plate while I watched. I could smell fried chicken in the kitchen. It was my favorite meal—or it would have been if it were homemade; I'd seen Molly stuffing the fast food containers into the trash can right before Dad got home—but for some reason tonight I couldn't stand the odor of it.

"Fine," I said, trying not to breathe in.

"Just fine?" Dad came in, carrying the chicken, and set a drumstick on my plate. "It's supposed to be the most advanced academic, high-tech wonder school—the only one of its kind—and all you can say is 'fine'?" He laughed and Molly kissed him as he walked past her. "Kids," he said, as if Molly knew anything about children. She'd never had any, and I'd heard her telling a friend on the phone she was glad she only had to be a mother to two of the darn things. Except she used a different word than *darn*.

Bryan wasn't having any problem eating, and he answered the question with his mouth full of mashed potatoes. "It was awesome! We had computer lab and played football at PE time. And my teacher, Ms. Morrigan, is the coolest."

"What about your teacher, Lorelei?" Dad asked.

"That's weird," I said. "My teacher is named Ms. Morrigan, too."

"Huh," Dad shrugged, not particularly interested. "What're

the odds of that?" He turned to me and scooped a forkful of carrots up to his mouth. One bitten piece fell off and landed on the purple tablecloth. I stared at it, a small orange crescent on the dark purple fabric, and felt my heart race like I was being chased by something huge, and I knew I couldn't run fast enough to escape.

"Lorelei? Did you make any new friends?" Dad looked annoyed. He probably thought I was being rude, just staring at the tablecloth. I guessed I was.

"Yeah. I met a kid named Andrew. And Allison's in my class."

He turned away, satisfied, before I even finished speaking. That was all he needed, just one little thing, and I was off the hook. He had a mental checklist: Come home from work? Check. Eat dinner? Check. Get Lorelei to tell about her day? Check. With me out of the way, he started talking to Bryan about football. Molly bustled around the table, fussing with the side plates and refilling Dad's, on her feet so much you would think she was allergic to chairs.

After dinner, Dad and Molly went to watch TV, leaving Bryan and me to clear up. "Hey, Bry," I said casually, "what do you really think about school?"

"What *would* I think?" He snapped a dish towel toward me and missed. "It's great. Now get in here and clean the counters, would you? I've got video games that need me."

Video games that needed him? I almost laughed. He was worried about video games, and I was worried about . . . what was I worried about?

"Hey," I said as he was closing the dishwasher, "how about a game of hide and seek?"

"What?" He looked up, surprised. We hadn't played that in years. But when we were younger, it was practically all we would do together. From the time I could talk, I would shout, "Count to a hundred" and run off, and Bryan would look for me for as long as it took. By the time I was six, I knew every hiding place in the neighborhood, but so did he.

"You want to play hide and seek?" he repeated and shook his head. "Sure, whatever."

It was almost a yes! "Count to a hundred," I yelled back, and ran out the door. I hid in the first place I found, behind the trash can. I knew he'd find me in less than a minute, but it didn't matter. I wanted to be found.

I stayed out there for a half hour, slapping at the mosquitoes that flew over to keep me company. It got darker and darker, and no one came calling. Dad and Molly probably didn't even know I was outside.

Bryan?

He had video games that needed him.

He wasn't looking for me. Nobody was.

It's all I deserve, I told myself.

I got up, knees stiff, and wandered back inside to my bedroom.

I couldn't remember falling asleep. But the next morning, I woke up with a wet pillow, and a sick, twisting hunger that felt like teeth chewing at my insides.

CHAPTER 8:

One Mouthful of Mystery

"Today, we will begin our study of Greek mythology," Ms. Morrigan said the next morning. One of the boys on the other side of the room raised his hand.

"Ms. Morrigan?"

It was Neil Ogden, this really mean kid from my neighborhood. I'd known him for a long time—he'd thrown rocks at me three years before, when I was selling Girl Scout cookies. Then he'd turned over our trash cans when I told my dad. Neil asked Ms. Morrigan a question with a really rude tone of voice, but his words were garbled. He swallowed a mouthful of candy and went on. "I think mythology's boring. Is everything in this school going to be boring?"

Ms. Morrigan smiled. "Neil, if you aren't interested in

today's topic, you can go to the library or the computer lab to entertain yourself until our morning recess. We'll be doing Candy Math again after that."

"I can leave?" Neil looked surprised. "I can just go?"

Ms. Morrigan nodded. "Of course. Next time, you needn't ask. Just excuse yourself. You'll find that children are the most important thing at Splendid. Not the lessons. The children themselves." She looked around. "Would anyone else like to go at this time? It would be best not to interrupt those students who are interested in our Greek mythology unit."

No surprise what happened then. Out of our class of fourteen kids, only seven stayed. Allison left with her new friends, all of them carrying their golden candy bowls in one hand and their cell phones in the other. None of the kids sitting nearby stayed, except for Andrew. I tried to get his attention, but he had his eyes shut. He was sweating, too, even though the room was cold. I knew why.

Ever since breakfast ended, I had been trying to avoid the candy dish. Today mine was filled with Skittles, because of my fictional lactose intolerance. I hated Skittles—they were so grainy, it felt like chewing sugar dirt—so it shouldn't have been a problem to keep from eating them. Plus, I had eaten at least four pieces of toast and three eggs at breakfast before the plates had been cleared. I had no reason to feel so hungry, but I had to sit on my hands to keep from stuffing my face with candy. The only reason I didn't get up and leave the classroom was that I didn't know if I could keep from eating if I didn't sit on my hands.

The concentration it took to ignore the golden bowl made it hard to stay in tune with what Ms. Morrigan was saying. When I finally wrenched my thoughts away from the candy, she was in the middle of her lecture, and most of the class was opening their books. "And so, each of you will be given the chance to choose from any of the figures in Greek mythology that interest you. Choose a favorite, if you have one. Or choose a minor figure, and write an additional myth to go along with the original. It's up to you. Be creative."

"Ma'am?" It was Andrew; he had his hand raised, but when the teacher frowned, he remembered and took it down. "Ms. Morrigan," he said, "can we work in pairs?"

"I suppose," she said. "You can assist each other. But I would prefer if each of you chose a different mythological character to research."

Andrew waved me over. I scooted my desk across the white tile floor. "Can we work together?" he asked.

"I don't write very well. It takes me a long time, and it's usually all jumbled up," I said after a few seconds. "I can't even read my own handwriting most of the time. Nobody ever wants to partner with me."

"That's okay," he said. "Nobody ever partners with me. But that's because I'm fat."

"That stinks," I said.

Andrew looked at me like I was a puzzle he couldn't solve.

"What?"

"How come you can't write well?" he asked.

"Because I'm dumb," I whispered back, and opened my book.

"No, you're not," he said. "You're the first one to get the math answers. And you can draw. I saw your sketch in art class. It was as good as a picture you would buy somewhere."

I blushed a little. I had drawn a unicorn, but I didn't know anyone had seen. My unicorns were pretty good, I guessed. Lots of practice and all. "It's just doodles."

"Whatever you say," he said, smiling. "I can't draw. My best subjects are science and lunch. So this year my mom sent me to science summer camp *and* fat camp. She's supportive that way." His T-shirt today was a blue one that said NUCLEAR PHYSICS IS THE BOMB. He patted his stomach right under the picture of a mushroom cloud.

I laughed, thinking how cool it was he could make fun of his own situation.

"So, why do you think you're dumb?"

I shrugged. "That's what my brother tells me."

"Sounds like a jerk."

"He wasn't always," I said. "We used to get along great. But then—" I stopped. I didn't want him to start looking at me the way kids always did when they found out your mom had died. They felt sorry for you, but they didn't want to come any closer in case it was contagious. Like Mom Death was a virus. "Something bad happened." My gut twisted, like I'd told a lie. Something bad had happened to Mom? More like *someone* bad.

Me.

"What?" he asked.

I didn't have to answer. Ms. Morrigan walked past and we opened our books, pretending to look for a character to research. My book fell open to a page with a picture of a mother and daughter embracing. The daughter looked a little like me. "Persephone," I murmured out loud. "Who's Persephone?"

Ms. Morrigan kneeled down next to my desk. "That's a wonderful choice, Lorelei. A very sad tale."

I looked into her flashing eyes and listened as she read the page out loud. "Persephone, the daughter of Demeter, the goddess of the hearth, was gathering narcissus buds on the hillside with her maidens. She was surpassingly fair, and thus attracted the attention of Hades, the God of the underworld, who decided to take her for his bride. He waited for the moment to present itself. At last, Persephone wandered too far from her maidens, and Hades tore through the underbelly of the earth, dragging her back down with him across the River Styx, and into the vault of the underworld itself."

"He was the god of what again?" I asked.

"The dead," Ms. Morrigan replied and went on. "When her mother realized what had happened, she left her temple, and wandered the countryside dressed in sackcloth, disguised as an old woman. Driven mad by grief, Demeter refused to bless the harvest, and the crops rotted in the fields. Winter came, and springtime was banished from the earth. The world cried out for food, but the grieving mother did not hear her stepchildren, desolate in the loss of her own dear daughter."

"Demeter was goddess of the harvest?" I asked. "So, without her, there was no food." My stomach growled, and I tried not to reach into the candy bowl.

Ms. Morrigan watched my fingers twitch, and smiled.

"Stubborn," she murmured.

"Me?" I asked. Was she talking about me?

But she shook her head. "Stubborn Demeter." She kept reading. "The other gods prevailed upon her to allow the springtime to come, lest all the earth perish. Hades agreed to let the kidnapped girl go back to her mother, but before she was allowed to return, she was to sit at the table in the feasting hall of the underworld. At dinner, Persephone ate six seeds of a pomegranate. When he saw this, Hades laughed, for she belonged to him. For each seed she took, she would spend one month each year with him in the underworld. The other half of the year she would return to her mother. And thus Demeter blesses the earth with spring and summer, and a good harvest, then mourns her daughter's loss for the length of every deep, dark winter."

"That's so sad," Andrew said. "To have to live in he—the underworld, I mean, for half the year?"

"Sad for the god Hades as well, I should think," Ms. Morrigan said, straightening up, "to live alone, waiting for his bride for six months of every year."

"But she wasn't his bride," I said. "He kidnapped her. He tricked her into eating the seeds, when he knew what would happen if she did it. She didn't want to be there; she didn't love him. Why would anyone feel sorry for him?"

Ms. Morrigan turned away, but I heard her answer. "Why, indeed? I merely point out, there are many sides to these old stories. Many ways to look at them. Even the villain in a play can bleed, and weep."

She walked quickly back to her desk and sat, thumbing

through some papers. She rested her forehead on one hand, hiding her face from view.

Andrew wiggled his eyebrows at me when he was sure she wasn't looking. "Okay, that was officially weird," he said. "I guess Ms. Morrigan's got issues with mythology."

I laughed softly. "Yeah. Well, one good thing: We don't have to read it now. But writing a new myth isn't going to be easy. Heck, sometimes writing the heading on my paper gives me a brain cramp."

"So do you know why you really have trouble writing?" Andrew asked. I looked up, checking to make sure he wasn't making fun of me. He wasn't; he just seemed interested.

"Yeah. I think I'm dysgraphic."

"What's that?"

"Kind of like dyslexic, except I can read fine. I just have trouble with the writing part of things." *A lot of trouble.*

"Oh. You only think you have it? Haven't you been tested or something?"

"No," I said. "My dad keeps saying we'll get around to it. I think he's hoping I'll grow out of it." I shrugged. "I do the best I can, and I keep my head down. Usually, the teachers give me Cs. Except in music and art. I get As in those. I was in choir at Russell Elementary. I wish we had music here. It's my best thing."

"You sing?" Andrew looked excited. "I love music. I've

played the piano for six years. I'm really good, I can even compose." He blushed. "I guess that sounded sort of conceited."

"No, it's okay," I said. "I love music, too. I can sing really well. I used to make up harmonies and sing with my . . ." I stopped. I couldn't talk about Mom.

But Andrew knew, somehow. "Your mom?" he asked. "I'm sorry."

"How did you—"

"I heard some other kids talking about it during art," he said. "I don't know anything else, just that she died last year. That's terrible."

"Thanks," I said, hoping he wouldn't say any more. He didn't.

After a few minutes, I looked back over. He was thumbing through the mythology book on his desk. "Which mythological person are you going to pick?" I asked.

"Orpheus," he said. "The guy who almost rescued his girlfriend from Hades, you know?" He stammered a little on the word *girlfriend*. "Since we get to rewrite the myth. I always wanted to write a happier ending to that one. Persephone's in it, too."

"You know all these stories already?"

He nodded. "I don't have a lot of friends, so I mostly just read. I have an old book like this at home."

We started brainstorming our new myths, with him

writing down the ideas. Even though he was doing most of the work, he didn't seem to mind. And he didn't make fun of my handwriting.

Just before free drawing time, Allison and the other girls came back from the library, their arms loaded up with the latest copies of some teen fashion magazines. She pulled me over to her group on the carpet. "Why do you hang out with him?" she asked, glaring at Andrew.

"I don't know. He's nice. He doesn't have any other friends."

"Well, you won't either if you keep talking to him all the time."

I was surprised; she sounded jealous. Maybe she'd forgotten that she was the one who'd stopped calling, stopped coming over, after Mom had gone to the hospital.

No, I reminded myself, *after I told her why Mom had to go to the hospital.* I didn't want to get into a fight, though, so I just said, "Ally. Come talk to him. He's cool."

She shuddered. "He's gross. And super fat."

That was so mean. I'd never heard her talk that way about anyone, not even in private. "Um, wrong side of the bed this morning?" I asked, and she rolled her eyes and changed the subject. Still, it made me mad. Who was she to talk? I almost pointed out the way her stomach was hanging over her jeans, but I didn't.

Ms. Morrigan was walking around the room, pushing the golden candy bowls closer to the students who were reading at their desks so they wouldn't have to reach as far to get their sugar fix. When she got to my desk and saw my untouched candy, I thought she was going to throw a fit, but she didn't. She just smiled to herself and nodded.

No, I wasn't going to make fun of Allison. I had a feeling that soon, I was going to need as many friends as I could get.

Recess was my favorite part of the day. No reading, no writing, no sitting still. The morning snack was pink cotton candy. I doused mine with water from my water bottle to make it disappear. Andrew sat on the swings, alone again, as usual. I hadn't realized until then how much being over-weight was like having some sort of contagious disease. No one played with him, or even talked to him, besides me. Sure, a few of the guys said hi, but when it was time for recess, they ran off with a football or played impossible games of chase and tag across the monkey bars that no kid Andrew's size could do.

I had asked Allison to swing, but she said she didn't want to mess up her hair. She'd reminded me so much of Molly I hadn't even argued. If she was going to turn into that kind of girl after all these years of being friends with me . . . well, she obviously wasn't going to want to hang out with me very much. I'd been feeling pretty sorry for myself, and lonely, until I'd seen Andrew waving me over to the swing set.

"Hey," I said, and got on the swing next to him. He was watching the eighth grade guys play football and laughing his head off. I looked and giggled as well. You've never seen anything funny until you've seen a bunch of guys playing football and carrying enormous cones of cotton candy at the same time. "Powder puff football, you think?" I asked.

Andrew just about fell off the swing laughing. "It does look like that, doesn't it? I wonder what game they'll play if our recess snack is pie?"

"Frisbee," I guessed. "With the empty pie tins, of course."

Andrew swiveled on his swing to look at me. His dark hair was sticking up in devil horns. It made him look really mischievous. "I've been thinking," he said.

"About what?" I asked. "And is it going to get us in trouble?"

"Ha," he said. "You'd have to murder someone to get in trouble at this school. I mean, the teachers let you do anything you want. Text, cut class, miss a homework assignment? No problem. As long as you eat, eat, eat." He laughed, but his eyes looked sad. "I know it's wrong, but I'm kind of looking forward to a bunch of these guys getting fat," he said. "Some of them live near me, and they've made fun of

me for years. Called me fatty, lardo. Even beat me up. But if they keep eating the way they have been, they're going to be the ones who are fat. And I'm not. I don't care how good the stupid food tastes. Nothing can possibly taste as good as revenge." His eyes were shining, and his voice had gotten loud, louder than I think he realized.

"Andrew, quiet down. They're gonna hear," I said, but just then Andrew flipped off the back of his swing. "Oh no!"

He hadn't fallen out of the swing; he'd been pulled. I looked behind me; six boys, Neil Ogden and Patrick from our class and four older boys, crowded around the empty swing and stared down at Andrew.

"Too late," one boy said. "We already heard."

Two of the older boys grabbed Andrew by the collar of his shirt and hauled him around to face them.

Patrick threw his empty cotton candy cone at Andrew's face. The sharp end hit right by his eye, but Andrew didn't move, only blinked.

"You ought to be more careful talking about people," Patrick said. "They might be standing right behind you." He kicked sand toward Andrew, who flinched. All the boys laughed.

"Yeah, what was that you said about not eating, anyway?" one of the kids holding him taunted. "A fatso like you? You know what I think?" He shook Andrew by the back of the neck. "I think you're so hungry, you'd eat anything. I think you'd eat dirt. Don't you think so, Neil?"

Neil scooped up a huge handful of the playground sand and held it up to Andrew's face. Andrew fought against the two boys holding him, but he couldn't get loose.

"Let me go!" he shouted, and twisted his arms, but the bigger boys just held tighter until he stopped struggling.

"Stop it!" I yelled. "Stop hurting him! He was just talking, he didn't mean anything."

Neil looked at me. "Don't get in the way, Lorelei, or you're next."

Neil was huge, and I had seen him beat up a girl before. I wouldn't stand a chance. I ran to get an adult, my feet slipping on the soft sand. I could hear Andrew choking behind me as the boys stuffed his mouth full of sand. What were they trying to do, suffocate him? My heart was pounding out of my chest as I swung through the doors to the cafeteria.

The room was empty except for a few of the waiters, who were sitting down on the soft chairs. I hadn't noticed before, but the wait staff all looked thin. Too thin, like pictures of anorexic people. Even their hair was thin. One of the girls was reaching for a cup of tea, and it shook as she lifted it. She spilled the tea all down her front when I caught my breath and yelled—"They're hurting him!"

Two of the guys stood up, alarmed.

"Already?" whispered the girl, her white shirt now covered with tea stains. She had a strange accent, and spoke each word slowly, precisely; her face twisted like it hurt to say each one. "But it's too soon."

"What?" I yelled. "What are you talking about? It's Andrew! The other boys are suffocating him!"

"Oh," she said, and sat back down. I noticed her mouth moving like she was chewing, or having to force each word out. "My friends? Can you . . . ?"

The two guys who had been sitting with her got up silently and walked out the doors with me. I pulled at their hands, trying to ignore how bony they felt—skeletal, even—as we went. "Hurry," I said. "Please. I wasn't kidding about the killing thing."

"Who's killing whom?" Principal Trapp was standing next to the swing set, patting Andrew on the back gently. She had a water bottle in her hand, and was giving him a small sip every few seconds. "Lorelei? Why have you brought the wait staff out here?"

She glanced at the waiters, who pulled their hands away from mine and backed up. "Gustav? Otto? Don't you have lunch to prepare?"

"Yes, ma'am," they murmured and shuffled away. I leaned down in front of Andrew.

"Andrew? Are you all right?"

He didn't say anything, but after a moment he coughed, and nodded weakly.

The principal spoke instead. "Poor Andrew, don't try to talk. Slipping out of the swing, what a shame. Well, for all that playgrounds are lovely, they can be dangerous if we're not careful." She patted him on the back one last time and handed him the rest of the water. "Finish this now, and watch yourself next time. I have high hopes for you, Andrew Fortner. Don't go choking to death before we can help you reach your potential." She stood up and looked at me.

"Principal Trapp," I said, straightening up as well. "He didn't fall. He was pushed. Those boys playing football now? Patrick and Neil, and some of the other guys—they were forcing him down, stuffing his mouth with sand."

"Is this true, Andrew?" She instantly looked concerned. "Did you eat the playground sand? That would be extremely . . . unhealthy. You might need medical attention."

"N-n-no," Andrew sputtered. "I told you. I slipped off the swing. The guys helped me up. Maybe Lorelei thought they pushed me."

I couldn't believe it. He was lying, bald-faced lying to her! And making me look like an idiot. I glared at him, and caught his wink.

"Maybe I was wrong," I muttered. "But it looked—"

"Now, Lorelei," she said sympathetically. "Don't get

overexcited. Boys play rougher than girls on the play-ground. You probably just misunderstood what was going on. Andrew is fine and he didn't say anything about boys pushing him down. Maybe you're feeling a bit . . . hungry, perhaps." She turned toward the cafeteria doors. "I'll have my staff make you some marzipan to go with your lunch."

As soon as she had gone back inside, I turned to Andrew and knelt down in front of him. He was still coughing softly.

"I'm sorry, Andrew. I couldn't stop them."

"It's . . . okay," he rasped out. "But . . . there's some-thing . . . wrong with the sand."

"What?" I asked. "Did they make you eat too much? Are you going to be sick?"

"No," Andrew said after taking a few seconds to breathe and cough. "But . . . can you grab some sand? You have a pocket or something? Put some in there and bring it inside. I need to find something out."

"Sure," I said. I pulled my paper cotton candy cone out of my pocket where I'd wedged it. "I'll fill this up. That way the sand won't spill out too much."

"Okay," Andrew wheezed and doubled over in another coughing fit.

Curious, I waited until he stopped, then asked, "Why are you interested in the sand?"

He looked up at me, and I could see the capillaries

around his eyes were broken, his eyes bloodshot from coughing so hard. "Lorelei," he said, after a few seconds, and paused. "I don't think . . . I don't think it's sand."

"What?"

At that moment, Ms. Morrigan called, "Time for Candy Math!" and the whole class ran past us, throwing their paper cotton candy cones to the ground as they went.

"I'll explain later," Andrew grunted. I helped him up, looking back at the field where the boys had been playing football. Their white cones littered the ground like unicorns' horns on some horrible, magical battlefield.

"Wow, Lorelei," I whispered to myself. "Your imagination's really running away with you."

Ms. Morrigan was standing at the door, her face twisted into a curious smile, and Andrew and I ran to catch up with the class.

Chapter 9:
Bright Sand, Dark Secret

Forty-five minutes later, Andrew and I sat alone in the science lab. As he lit the Bunsen burner in front of us with a match, I was overcome by how different this school was from any other school I'd ever been to, and how wrong.

"Messed up," I said out loud.

"What?" Andrew looked up at me, brown eyes sparkling as brightly as the sand he was pouring into the small metal tool in his hand. It was like a miniature scientific version of one of those toys little kids play with in the sandbox: a sifter. The pieces of sand were just big enough not to fall through the tiny holes in it.

"I was just thinking," I said. "About this. I mean, this is really dangerous. That's a torch. An open flame!"

He laughed at me. "Oh, no! An open flame! Don't worry, Lorelei. I'm a Boy Scout." He looked back down at the sifter, muttering, "Open flame, what will we do?" and chuckling.

"Fine, laugh at me. I don't care. But we're still kids. We could burn ourselves up—or the whole school down. Hey, look at what happened at the other middle school." I wondered if I should mention the creepy thing Ms. Morrigan had said about the kitchen ovens being left on. "Do you think it really was wiring?"

"I guess it must have been. I mean, no one was in the building, right? Still, schools don't usually burn down like that. They have all sorts of sprinkler systems, alarms . . ." His voice trailed off as he studied the sand.

"Well, be careful. You say you told Ms. Morrigan what we were doing?"

"Not precisely. I told her we were going to run an experiment. All she said was we needed to be back in time for lunch. Of course."

"Oh. I still can't believe kids can just come and go. It's cool, sure, but it's strange too. They're not taking care of us. The only thing they seem to worry about is—"

"How much we eat," Andrew said. "Yeah, I had a grandma who did that. She used to pile my plate up over and over, and if I told her I was full, she would cry and ask if I didn't love her."

"Weird," I said. "So is that how . . ." I stopped. I didn't want to ask about his weight; he'd already had a really bad day.

"Yeah, part of the reason I got fat." He shook the sand in the sifter and lowered it close to the flame. "Of course, my genes didn't help. We're fat in my family for at least four generations. Big bones, too. I had to live with Grandma for two years, when Mom had cancer. That's when I got so fat, and I couldn't lose it. Not that a five-year-old knows how to diet."

"Your mom had cancer?" I asked. "Is she . . . okay?"

"Yeah, she's in remission," Andrew said. "Six years now."

"What kind of cancer was it?"

Andrew blushed. I couldn't figure out why until he said it. "You know. Breast cancer."

"Oh," I said. "That's good. Breast cancer's really curable these days."

I was thinking about my mom and her death. Andrew had told me about his mom's cancer. Maybe I should tell him about my mom? I hadn't told anyone except Allison. *Yeah, because when you did tell her what happened, she dropped you like a brick, idiot.*

But Andrew's mom had had it, too. Maybe he would understand. Maybe he wouldn't act like it was contagious. He would know better.

His voice interrupted my thoughts. "What happened to

your mom?" he murmured, shaking the crystals over the flame. They were starting to spark a little, a few of them catching fire so close to the torch.

"She died," I whispered and cleared my throat. The familiar stabbing pain near my heart started up when I said it, and I crossed my arms over my chest.

"I know, but how?" Andrew asked. "If you can talk about it."

"I've only told one person. And then she sort of . . . stopped hanging around when I did. So I never talk about Mom."

Andrew looked up. "You don't talk about your mom?" He frowned. "Why not?"

I took a breath. I didn't have to tell him everything. But I could tell him some of it. "She was killed."

His jaw dropped. "Murdered, you mean?" He looked horrified.

"Not exactly. She had an accident. Someone made her fall. She had cancer, so when she fell it made her legs break. She went to the hospital. But she never came home."

"I'm sorry. I don't get it, though. She didn't die of cancer? She died of falling? Who pushed her, anyway?" His eyes were dark and sympathetic, and I almost told him.

But it hurt too much. "I don't want to talk about it."

He didn't speak for a few seconds, just looked at me,

ignoring the sand that had ignited in the sifter. I was afraid he had guessed it—that I was the one who had made her fall—but he didn't say anything. He just asked, in a quiet voice, "What kind of cancer did she have?" But before I could answer he said the word that was on my lips. "Bone!"

"What?" I said. "How did you know?"

"Know what?" Andrew looked confused.

"That my mom had . . . that kind of cancer. Did Allison tell you? No one else even knew."

"Oh, no. I didn't know. I'm sorry about that. Bone cancer is awful." He shook his head and looked back down at the sifter, where the sand was turning to ash. "I meant that the sand isn't sand. It's bone." He turned white and swallowed hard. "I can't believe I ate this stuff."

"How do you know it's not sand?" I asked, peering at the crystals. "It looks like sand to me."

"But watch it burn," he said, and sprinkled some more sand on top of the wire mesh. I watched as it caught fire and sparked, then burned away.

"So?"

"It burns a little blue," Andrew whispered. "Sand doesn't burn, and stone doesn't burn blue. Only bone—well, some kinds of bone—do that."

"How do you know that?"

"Science summer camp, remember? We did a forensics unit." He wrinkled his nose. "And smell. It smells wrong."

I leaned down to sniff. He was right. It didn't smell like any campfire I had ever smelled before. What it did smell like was the oven when Dad had forgotten a rack of lamb in it for four hours and gone out to do yard work. When I'd come back into the house from playing outside, smoke had been pouring out of the oven, and that had been the smell. Burned bone.

"I don't understand," I said, backing up. "Why would the playground sand be . . . that? And all ground up? Where would they even get that much to begin with? That's crazy."

Andrew looked at me, measuring me with his eyes. "Crazy? Maybe," he said. "Or maybe something else. Worse than crazy."

"What kind is it?" I wondered aloud. "Where would you even get that much . . ." I didn't say the word—I never said it—but the thought hung in the air between us, like poisoned smoke, and for a moment, neither one of us took a breath.

Bone?

The bell rang then, and it was time for lunch.

I was so distracted by the thought that the playground sand was ground-up bone pieces that I forgot to stop eating.

When lunch was finished, Ms. Morrigan walked over from the seventh-grade table she'd been sitting at and smiled at me, smug and dismissive. "Seems you were hungry today, little Lorelei," she said. "I knew you would eat eventually. I told her you were no different."

No different? I felt different; I felt sick. I looked down. My plate had been taken away already, and I couldn't remember what I'd eaten, but the inside of my mouth felt slick and greasy, coated with butter and oil. I sniffed my fingers; they smelled like almonds.

Marzipan, I remembered. I had eaten tray after tray of marzipan. My stomach was so full it almost felt crampy, so I got up slowly and wandered down the hallway to the restroom instead of back to class. I stood in the stall, facing the toilet, wondering if I was going to throw up—kind of hoping I would, just to stop my stomachache—when I heard the door open and voices.

"So, my teacher, Ms. Morrigan, is the coolest. She lets us eat candy all day long, and she never makes us raise our hands." It was Tess, one of the girls from my class.

Another voice answered, but I didn't recognize it. "That's so weird. My teacher's name is Ms. Morrigan, too. Do you think they're sisters or something?"

"Maybe, I don't know," Tess replied. I heard them go into the stalls, but they never stopped talking.

"Oh my gosh, Tess, I am getting so fat! I can hardly button my jeans!"

"Me, too. I totally need to go on a diet. But the food here is so awesome. It's better than the stuff I get at home."

"I know what you mean. My mom doesn't even cook anymore, anyway. It's all fast food burgers and frozen dinners. They take better care of us here than our parents do. You know, our teacher has a whole bowl of Tums in the classroom, if your stomach hurts. I could get you one."

"I'll have to ask Ms. Morrigan for some. You know what? I wish I could live here all the time." Tess laughed, and their toilets flushed.

"Yeah, that would be paradise."

A part of me agreed with them. If it weren't for the creepy things I kept discovering—and the strange feeling I had that there was something secret, something really bad, that none of us kids had figured out—I would want to live here, too.

For a minute, I was jealous of those girls. And mad at Andrew. If he hadn't stopped me from eating those M&M's, if he hadn't showed me the bone sand, I would be happy. I would be just like those other girls, excited about all the cool things at the school.

Of course, I knew that wasn't true. I would never be like

Tess and her friend. Those girls hadn't done the thing I had done. They still had moms to go home to.

The familiar loneliness rushed over me, and I ran back into the stall to get some toilet paper. I didn't want Ms. Morrigan to see me crying.

When I walked out of the bathroom, sniffling, Principal Trapp was there, pinning something to a bulletin board.

"Lorelei!" She whirled around and dropped the tacks she was holding. I bent and scooped them up, handing them back carefully. "You surprised me!" She leaned down to see my face. "You've been crying."

I started to interrupt her, tell her I had just been washing my face, but she held up a hand.

"Don't worry. I'm not going to ask you about it. Everyone has secrets. Yours are as dark as anyone's, aren't they? They're yours to keep. You don't need to tell anyone, not your friends. Not me."

"Thanks," I said, wondering if she really understood. Something in her stare reminded me of the way my eyes had looked for those long months after Mom died. Maybe Principal Trapp did understand. Maybe she had done something just as horrible, something she never thought she would do.

"Will you help me pin this up?" she asked, and handed me a tack.

"Sure," I answered automatically and helped straighten the poster board she was working on.

It was a giant green sign, and I read it while she unfolded the stepladder.

MUSIC CLASS BEGINS THURSDAY! PLEASE WELCOME MS. THRENODY.

"Music starts Thursday?" I asked. "As in, the day after tomorrow?"

She nodded, and I yelled, "Woo-hoo!"

My shout and then her laughter echoed down the hall.

"I don't know if all the students will be as happy to lose their extra recess!" She climbed up the ladder to fix the top corners of the poster.

"Probably not," I agreed. "It's just that music is my favorite class."

"I can tell. I hope you like her. I've known her for years. She's one of the most talented musicians I've ever heard. Actually, she reminds me of you. Smart, musical, perceptive . . . and beautiful. And her voice is mesmerizing." She looked at me with a grin and stuck one final tack in the poster. "Of course, I've heard yours is something special, too."

"Oh, I don't sing anymore," I said, feeling my face heat. "Not since . . . well, not for a long time." I hesitated. "I used to sing for my mom."

"I would love it if you would sing for me, Lorelei," the principal said, climbing down.

"Oh, I couldn't," I began, but stopped when she placed her hand on my shoulder. She smiled straight into my eyes. "Are you going to make me ask pretty please?" she teased.

Before I could think better of it, I sang. I didn't exactly choose it, but the first song that came to mind was one my mother had taught me. One we had sung together for years.

"*When I was just a little girl, I asked my mother, what will I be?*" I broke off, embarrassed. The next part was supposed to be a duet, with my mom on the high descant.

The principal whispered the chorus by herself. "*Que sera, sera. Whatever will be, will be . . .*" Her voice trailed off, too.

"Lorelei is the perfect name for you. Siren song," she said quietly. "Has anyone ever told you that your voice is almost magical?"

My mom had said that. Right then, the principal reminded me so much of my mom, I couldn't answer her. I was afraid I might cry. I nodded once.

"Ms. Threnody will fall in love with you." Still smiling, she patted me on the shoulder. "Now off to class."

"Principal Trapp." I had almost forgotten the sand.

"Yes?"

"It's probably dumb, I know," I said, rushing to get the words out, "but I was wondering about the playground. About the sand."

"The sand?" She looked utterly confused. "I'm not sure—ah! Alva. There you are. I wondered when you would notice one of your chicks had fallen out of the nest."

I felt a frigid hand on my arm, and looked down. Ms. Morrigan's nails were sharp at the tips, and they looked like pale claws against my tanned skin.

"I was worried, Lorelei," Ms. Morrigan said, but I could tell from her expression she wasn't. She was angry. "I've been looking everywhere."

Principal Trapp laughed. "Don't be too hard on her. She was helping me with the bulletin board. It's my fault."

Ms. Morrigan, her hand still on my arm, turned toward her classroom, shaking her head so hard I thought her braids might come undone. "Let's go."

Principal Trapp winked at me, and then made a face behind Ms. Morrigan's back. I almost laughed.

Ms. Morrigan pulled me down the hallway until we turned a corner. Then she stopped, and wrenched me around to face her.

"Ouch!"

"You were asking about the sand. Why?"

The question crackled in the air between us. I didn't want to answer, I knew that. I wanted to tell her to stuff it . . . but her eyes narrowed, and my head filled with static. I heard a voice—my voice—from blocks away, hissing through clenched teeth.

"Andrew."

Narrower slits of blue flashed with victory. "Andrew did what?"

Each word burned in my mouth. "Said . . . the sand . . . was . . . really . . ."

"Go on. Say it."

She stared into my eyes, and I could feel the word buzzing to be let out. But, even with a mind gone fuzzy, even with her eyes flickering like summer lightning, I knew I couldn't say that word. It was my secret, my deepest secret. Principal Trapp's voice echoed in my mind. *Your secrets are as dark as anyone's, aren't they? They're yours to keep. You don't need to tell anyone.*

I didn't have to answer completely. But those eyes demanded a word. "Strange," I answered at last, and felt my mind buckle under Ms. Morrigan's gaze.

You won't remember the sand.

I won't remember the sand.

You won't talk to Andrew.

I won't talk to Andrew.

You will avoid him.

I will.

You're hungry. You will eat.

My stomach growled an answer, and that part of my mind that had questioned, that had seen the strangeness around me, crumbled into dust.

CHAPTER 10:
Force-Fed

On Wednesday, no matter what I did, Andrew wouldn't leave me alone. I'd avoided him for the rest of Tuesday. It wasn't difficult. He'd seemed preoccupied with something, like he was thinking as hard as he could. But the next day was harder. I tried ignoring him, avoiding him in the hallways, even asking Ms. Morrigan to let me join the girls' group for our mythology study. He kept pestering me, though. Finally, right after lunch, he grabbed my arm, stopping me from going back to class.

"Andrew," I hissed. "What's your problem? Let me go!"

"What's happened?" he asked, keeping his voice low, too. "I've been watching you all day. You've been eating. A lot."

The wait staff was clearing the last plates from the table, and one of them—Gustav? Otto?—looked at us curiously.

"Come outside with me, Lorelei. Now, before Ms. Morrigan notices we're gone," he said, and tried to pull me toward the door.

"What in the world? No, Andrew. I'm not going anywhere with you. Let me go!"

His fingers tightened, and I pulled back harder.

He stopped squeezing when he realized I was serious, but he didn't let go. "What happened, Lorelei? You're different. Something happened after lunch yesterday."

He was speaking slowly, like I was stupid. It made me want to scratch his eyes out. Bryan talked to me that way sometimes, when he wanted to really make me mad. "Yesterday, you left the cafeteria and you were gone for a long time. Where did you go? Who did you see?"

"Andrew Fortner, I am going to kick you in the privates if you don't let me go right this instant," I said. "I'm not stupid. I didn't see anyone yesterday. I just went to the bathroom."

Andrew backed up, worried I really was going to kick him, I guess. "Calm down, Lorelei. I know you're not stupid. I just want to know where you went. Who you saw. Was anyone in the bathroom?"

I thought back. Why did my thoughts seem blurred again? Maybe I had a brain tumor. Maybe I was just being annoyed to death. Either way, I wanted to get back to class. I was hungry, and Ms. Morrigan had brought a snow-cone maker into the classroom as a special treat for working hard on our math lesson.

"Fine. I ran into Tess and some other girl. They talked about their teachers, and then they left. Then I went back to class." I pulled against his hand again. "Now let me go. I will tell Principal Trapp about this, you know. You'll get thrown out of school, and I won't care."

"You won't?" he said, looking at me like I'd just kicked him for real.

"No, I won't," I said. "It'll just mean more food for the rest of us, fatso."

"Lorelei!" He gasped. Was he going to cry? Maybe. A thought flashed through my mind, like a diver rising to the surface for a quick breath—How could I say that? What was happening to me?—but then it went away, and I pulled free of his hands at last.

"Wait." I had almost left the room, when his voice stopped me. It sounded . . . broken. I looked back. He was crying, one tear inching down his cheek, his arms wrapped around himself.

"I'm listening."

"If you come with me right now, I'll leave. I promise. I'll leave the school and never come back. I already asked my parents if I could transfer out. They said no, but I could convince them." He lifted the bottom of his shirt up and rubbed the hem across his eyes to dry them. "You'll never have to see me again. But I want you to do one thing for me."

"I'll never have to see you again? Quick, tell me," I said. He was crying harder now. I had caused those tears. "What do you want me to do?"

It was probably a trick. He was trying to get me into trouble. I told him that.

"How could you possibly get into trouble at Splendid?" he answered calmly, sniffing. "There aren't any rules here. You can go anywhere you want, do anything you want to, remember?"

I thought he was wrong—I knew there was something wrong with what he was saying—but I just nodded. I wanted to get rid of him, get him out of my life, so I could go back to class, and my friends, and the golden dish that my teacher kept full of candy for me. My stomach twisted. I was starving. I needed to get rid of him so I could grab a snack.

"Fine," I said. "I'll come. For one minute. Then you disappear, and never come back."

"Agreed," he said, looking sadder than ever.

I followed him outside, squinting at the glare of the sunshine on the white sand of the playground.

Sand. It was sand, wasn't it? For some reason, I couldn't

remember why, I had a feeling it was something else. Something scary.

Andrew's fault, I thought. A breeze whistled past, and the leaves on the tree nearby rustled a warning. *Stop listening to him. Get away from him. He's trying to ruin your life.*

Andrew had crossed over to the jungle gym, reached down into the sand, and returned before I could decide to leave.

"Here, Lorelei. Do you remember what this is?"

Go back inside, the leaves rustled. *Be safe.*

My hair whipped around my face as the wind grew stronger. "It's sand," I said. "It's playground sand. Is that all?"

He tilted his head. "You don't remember? Our science experiment? Yesterday, when we snuck into the science wing and burned the sand?"

"No," I said. "I don't. And the wind is messing up my hair. Can I go now?"

"Yeah, sure," Andrew said. "After you do one thing. One little thing."

"What?" I was really suspicious now. I knew there had to be a catch.

"Eat it," he said. And he held his hand—full of sand—up to my face.

I couldn't help it; I backed up a step. "You want me to eat sand? You're crazy!"

"Okay, crazy. I can live with that. I've been called worse." He looked down at his stomach.

"No," I said. "I'm not going to do it. I'd throw up. You're completely demented."

"Eat one piece, then," Andrew said. "Just one. That couldn't possibly make you throw up. And you'll see why I asked you."

"One piece?" I asked. "And you'll leave me alone?"

Andrew held up one hand in what had to be a Boy Scout salute. "On my honor. One piece, and if you don't see what I mean, I'll leave forever. You'll never have to see me again."

"Fine," I said. I reached out, took a grain of sand off his palm, and put it on my tongue. It tasted strange—bitter, then sweet, harsh and sugary in turns. It tasted like tears and terror and . . . "Marzipan?"

Andrew was looking at me as if he expected something to have changed. "How do you feel, Lorelei? Can you remember what happened yesterday now? Do you remember . . . any of it?"

I didn't answer. My mouth was parched, the sand wicking away every bit of moisture as it sat on my tongue. Sand didn't do that, I knew. Sand didn't change taste or turn your mouth as dry as . . . I shook my head and tried to spit, but my mouth felt like a desert.

"After I swallowed it," Andrew whispered, glancing at

the doors, "things started to make sense. You'll see. You'll be able to . . . think about what's going on, now."

"What are you talking about?" I said. "I feel like an idiot, if that's what you mean. But I did it. I ate your stupid sand. Now leave me alone," I shouted. "Leave the school. Never come back."

Andrew started to cry again, and I felt sick, like my stomach was turning inside out. I shouldn't care, but strangely, I did. Why didn't I hate him? He was disgusting, and rude, and annoying. So why did his tears hurt like they were my own?

"I guess one piece wasn't enough," he whispered. He opened his hand and stared at the rest of the sand.

"What did you expect to happen, Andrew?" I hesitated, my back to him, for a moment ignoring the leaves that rustled for me to run inside, get away, stop listening. He didn't answer, though, and I took a few steps toward the door.

Tight, gripping fingers on my arm stopped me again. I couldn't believe it.

"What in the—"

I spun around on my heel, mouth open, ready to tell him exactly what I thought of him grabbing me. Instead, I found my open mouth stuffed full of sand, and his hand grinding it in, forcing my jaw shut.

I tried to scream and pull away, but all I succeeded

in doing was swallowing a mouthful of the hateful, bitter stuff, and breathing in enough to make my lungs explode with pain. Each grain was a spark, burning me from the inside out.

Andrew let me go, and I fell to the ground. *Why had he done this?* I closed my eyes against the pain of the sand in my lungs.

When I opened them, Andrew had run away.

Someone must have heard my coughing because one of the kitchen workers ran out and helped me inside. In less than a minute, I was sitting in an office I'd never seen before, lying on a green velvet sofa, and trying not to cough. It felt like my throat was bleeding. Then the door opened.

It was Bryan, and he looked scared.

"Lorelei? Lorelei, are you okay?"

My brother's voice was quieter, and kinder, than I'd heard in years.

"Not really," I tried to speak, but no sound came out. I cleared my throat, and fire shot through my chest. I doubled over, my lungs burning. Bryan helped me lie back on the sofa. After a few seconds of coughing, I opened my eyes again.

Bryan was sitting on a chair with legs carved into the shapes of fish, each one a little different from the others. I stared at one of the fish—a salmon?—for a few seconds,

catching my breath. I wondered where you get chairs with those kinds of legs. They looked hand-carved.

"They are hand-carved," a strange voice answered my thoughts. Had I spoken out loud? I looked up.

A lady stood in front of me, smiling. Her teeth were as white as seashells and her eyes were the silver-gray of the ocean during a storm. She was terribly thin, like she hadn't eaten a solid meal in months. She wore a long silver skirt and a white blouse that made me think of the foam-capped breakers I'd seen at the beach with Mom and Dad years before.

"My name is Ms. Threnody," she said, her voice rich and soft, like caramel melting.

I wondered where she was from. I wanted to ask her to keep talking, so I could hear her accent, but my throat hurt too much. Bryan spoke up. "You're the new music teacher?"

"Yes," she said, and faced him. "My, you are a handsome boy. Bryan, is it?"

He nodded, and turned red. He liked her; he was making the same moony face he had the summer before around the high school cheerleader who lived two doors down.

Ms. Threnody reached out and touched his arm. "Tell me, Bryan. Do you enjoy music class?"

I knew Bryan had always hated music class, but I had the feeling he was going to lie, tell her he loved it. I closed my eyes.

"No," Bryan said, and blushed. "I mean, yes." He swallowed. "I don't know why I said that. I mean to say, I really, *really* . . . hate music class."

My jaw dropped. Bryan wasn't usually this honest . . . or this stupid-sounding.

Ms. Threnody raised one eyebrow. "Really? What a shame. And I was so looking forward to teaching you." She started to move away. Bryan reached out and touched her skirt and she stopped.

"I'll come to music," he said. "Maybe I'll, um, appreciate it more with you for my teacher."

"That would be lovely," she replied and turned the door handle. "Lorelei? I'll need you to answer some questions about what happened on the playground after your throat feels a bit better."

When she left, it was as if all the air had been sucked out of the room. I took a deep breath, ready to tease my brother, but regretted it. My lungs felt like they were lined with splinters. Bryan smacked his hand against his head.

"I can't believe I said that."

I struggled to take a breath and rasped out, "Yeah. Smooth . . . move . . . Ex . . . Lax."

Bryan laughed, but then he stopped, shaking his head. "It was the weirdest thing. I didn't mean to say that. I wasn't going to tell her I hated music. It just . . . came out. Like in those spy movies, where they inject the guy with truth serum." He paused. "Did you see her eyes? I've never seen eyes so . . . deep."

I wanted to tease my brother about Ms. Threnody's truth-inducing eyelashes, when I remembered.

"Andrew." I whispered the name, then coughed into my hand. I felt a tear slip down my face from the pain, and looked into my hand, sure there would be blood there, though there wasn't. I had to know. "Andrew?"

"That jerk the waiters saw shoving your face into the

sand?" Bryan asked. "What a freak. They caught him trying to run away from school. Ms. Morrigan took care of him. They disappeared into the principal's office right when I got here—oh, she tried to call Dad and Molly, but their phones must be off or something, so I'm all the family you got."

I wasn't surprised that Molly wasn't answering her phone. Most mothers watch their phones for the school phone number. I had a feeling she turned hers off the minute we walked out the front door. But I didn't want to think about her right now, or Dad. I was worried about Andrew.

"Why'd that kid start messing with you, anyway? You give him a hard time 'cause he's such a slob?"

I shook my head. I had been so cruel to Andrew. I knew he'd hurt me with the sand, but he'd had a reason. I couldn't remember exactly what—but it was coming back to me in flashes. Something about food, and bones.

Bone. A secret Andrew knew. That I had known. Why couldn't I remember?

"Andrew?" I asked again, ignoring the fire in my windpipe. "Where?"

Bryan shrugged, and pulled a handful of candy out of his pocket. "I dunno. Still in with her, I guess. I wouldn't be surprised if they kicked him out of Splendid. It's not public school, you know. They don't have to keep him." He held out a handful of candy. "Want one?"

It was so bizarre to have Bryan being nice, talking to me, that I didn't even hesitate. I grabbed a few of the candies and popped them in my mouth, unthinking. When I swallowed, the cracked chocolate shells sliding down my throat felt like broken glass. "Ouch," I whispered.

"You should have seen your teacher going off on that kid." Bryan kept stuffing his face, talking through the chewing sounds. "If she hadn't already decided to eat Andrew alive, I'd do it for her."

Eat Andrew alive? For some reason, those words rang in the back of my mind.

Something was wrong at Splendid Academy. Something that had to do with the food, and how much the kids were eating. Something no one would ever suspect. And I had a wild, crazy idea that I knew what it was, and who was responsible.

As if I had summoned her there with my thoughts, Ms. Morrigan walked in, tapping a stick across her palm.

I wanted to scream, but it hurt. Bryan let out a yell for me. "A stick?!"

CHAPTER 11:
Suspicion

The stick was small and plain, just a sanded-down tree branch, but in my teacher's hand it looked like a weapon.

"Are you kidding?" Bryan jumped up, smiling. "You beat that jerk with a stick? Awesome. Wait until I tell the guys."

Ms. Morrigan's laughter chimed, but it sounded angry. "Beat Andrew? Of course not. That wouldn't be very progressive, now would it? What would the principal say?"

They both laughed like she had told a great joke.

Bryan gave her a thumbs-up. "I guess Lorelei's going to be okay. Other than the not talking thing. Kind of nice for a change. But I hope that kid got his. She is my sister and all.

I don't want anyone else beating her up. That's my job." He gave me a quick side hug, and they laughed again.

I cleared my throat, ignoring the shooting pain the sound produced. Bryan asked for me. "Is Molly coming to pick her up?"

"We've tried to reach her," Ms. Morrigan said slowly. "We've left messages at home and on her cell. I'm sure she'll get back to us soon."

"Well, she's useless. Try Dad again," Bryan said. "He'll come, even if she won't."

Ms. Morrigan shook her head. "It's you I'm worried about. Don't you need to get back to class? Lorelei will be fine. It was just a little sand." She shooed him toward the door. "Hurry now, or you'll miss afternoon snack."

When Bryan left, Ms. Morrigan sat down next to me on the green chair.

"Feeling better?" she asked, her smile dropping away as soon as the door swung shut.

"Where's . . . Andrew?"

"Oh, your little friend? You don't need to worry about him anymore. I—what's the expression you kids use?—oh, yes. I really chewed him out."

She smiled wider, and I thought I saw something—a bit of salad? Or was it a strand of dark hair?—stuck between her front teeth. She ran her tongue over her teeth, and touched the corner of her mouth lightly with a fingertip, as if she were wiping the tiniest bit of chocolate away.

No one would ever believe me, but I had a feeling I knew exactly what had happened to him.

I was afraid I might throw up, and I was plain old afraid as well, as scared as I had ever been in my life. There was no one to help me here, no parents at home to call. No adult who cared about me, except maybe . . .

"P-p-p-principal Trapp," I managed, and the door swung open again. Like magic, the principal walked in, and I heaved a silent sigh of relief.

The teacher couldn't hurt me, not with her boss right there. I had to get Ms. Morrigan out of the room, though, so I could tell the principal what I suspected.

No, Lorelei, I reminded myself. *You can't tell anyone what you suspect. Because it's crazy.* Ugh. I hated it when my inner voice spoke up, and was right.

Principal Trapp smiled gently at me. "Alva, dear, thank you so much for your concern. I can handle this now. You had better get back to class."

Mission accomplished and I hadn't even spoken a word. Ms. Morrigan left, but she didn't seem happy about it. Principal Trapp turned to me, her face creased with worry. I must have looked really bad.

"You have had an exciting day, haven't you, dear?" she said, shaking her head slightly. She reached for me and I smelled the same perfume Ms. Morrigan wore. Lilies. I couldn't help it; I flinched. Her hand stopped and hovered over my forehead, then settled on my hair, lightly stroking a stray piece behind my ear.

"Rest now," she murmured. I coughed again, trying to act like I had just been responding to some sand in my airway.

Sand, I thought, my mind going fuzzy for a minute. Sand didn't feel like that, didn't stick to the inside of your mouth, to your windpipe. It wasn't sand in my throat at all.

"A-Andrew?" I managed, feeling dizzy. Maybe I had imagined it. Maybe Ms. Morrigan hadn't gotten him? I had to ask, even if my throat bled from the effort. Had to warn Principal Trapp, somehow. "Wh-wh-whe—"

"Yes, I need to ask you about that. He said you tripped, and that he was helping you. But the wait staff said something different. They said he was hurting you. Which was it, Lorelei? You can tell me."

"Not . . . on . . . purpose . . ." My lungs exploded with fire again as the words set off another wave of coughing.

Principal Trapp stroked my hair, over and over, and I felt my eyes closing. *No*, I thought, *I can't sleep. I have to tell her.* I heard her voice. "Hush, now. It doesn't matter. I'll stay with you. I won't leave you."

I slept until Molly got there, a few minutes before the end of the school day. I couldn't talk, couldn't tell anyone what I suspected. That night, I tried to write it down, but writing was harder than ever, and I was tired from coughing and from listening to Dad and Molly yell about who was supposed to pick me up if I "got sick" again. I stayed in my room through dinner and fell asleep crying. I dreamed of chocolate brown eyes that became candies, and a dinner party where all the plates were heaped with sand.

CHAPTER 12:
Nothing Special

A ndrew wasn't at school the next day. His empty desk distracted me from everything else. I tried to work on our mythology report, but the words kept getting mixed up when I wrote them. Ms. Morrigan, who I'd thought couldn't care less about whether or not her students did any real schoolwork, kept peeking over my shoulder, checking up on me.

I wasn't about to tell her about my dysgraphia. So I told her I couldn't concentrate, that I needed more protein. While she went to the cafeteria to get me some nuts, I sneaked a peek into Andrew's desk. His books and papers were all still there.

I wanted to think he was out sick, or that he'd just been

sent home—suspended, if they even do that at a charter school—for a while. If he was gone for good, wouldn't they have cleaned out his desk? He had to come back. Because if he didn't, if he couldn't, if what I had imagined was true . . .

I barely made it to the bathroom before I was sick. I stayed there with my head pressed against the cold white basin for a half hour, my stomach roiling.

Allison and her pack of new friends were waiting for me on the playground at recess.

"So, what happened with that kid Andrew? Did he really try to kill you?" She took a big bite of the caramel apple in her hand. I'd already "dropped" mine in the sand. I wasn't hungry.

"Where'd you hear that?" I asked. "He wasn't doing anything like that."

"Your brother told everyone he was trying to suffocate you. I heard you almost died." She was looking at me strangely, the way mean little kids look at a butterfly with one wing gone, flapping around on the ground. A little sympathetic, but mostly curious. Will it fly? Will the other wing fall off?

"Bryan doesn't know what went on. He wasn't here." I pointed to the spot where I had talked to Andrew. "I tripped on the edge of the jungle gym and fell. I hit my head. Maybe I was suffocating on the sand." I coughed for effect. "I know

I breathed some in. It really hurt. Andrew pulled my head up. He probably saved my life."

She narrowed her eyes. "What were you doing out here, anyway, Lorelei? Just you and him." She shot a look at the other girls, and they all smiled the same, sly smile. "Were you and Andrew . . . kissing?"

"Oh my gosh! Why would you even think that? That's totally not how I feel about Andrew."

"Oh, how you 'feel' about Andrew?" she repeated. "So, you admit you have feelings for the guy? Lorelei, you could have just told me. I am your friend, after all. Or I was before you met Andrew."

My face burned. "Well, you sure aren't being one right now," I said. I didn't say the other thing I was thinking, that she'd stopped being my friend a long time before I met Andrew. Not once I made the mistake of telling her my secret.

Still, I couldn't afford to lose another friend. "Just drop it, okay? I'll tell you about it later. Maybe you could spend the night—"

"No, I want to know now," she said, and took a step closer to me. "We all do, right?"

The other girls nodded.

"How is it, exactly, that you 'feel' about Andrew? Do you like him? Or are you just messing with him, giving the fat kid hope?"

I wanted to talk to her alone, but I could tell that wasn't going to happen. It was almost time to go back in; in fact, the older kids were rushing past us, moving from the football field to the doors in a noisy herd.

My throat hurt, but I had to raise my voice to be heard.

"You don't get it. I don't think about Andrew that way. He's like—a brother, I guess. But a nice brother." I smiled, knowing Allison would remember what I was talking about. She'd seen Bryan at his worst. "Not a jerk like Bryan. Get it?"

Someone shoved me in the back, knocking me down. I twisted around, wondering if Andrew had come back to make me eat more sand. But it wasn't Andrew standing there behind me, looking furious.

It was Bryan.

"Harsh, Lorelei. You're such a—" and he called me a name he had never used before. He kicked a little sand over my jeans before he ran past me.

Allison looked down at me with a sad expression. "You shouldn't be so mean to your brother. He's your family. And I would think you especially would know how important it is to be good to your family."

I felt like she'd punched me in the stomach.

"Ally?" I whispered.

She just tilted her head again. "Just sayin', Lorelei. Just sayin'."

She threw her apple core and stick onto the sand and followed her group of friends into the school.

Great. I'd ticked off my brother, and the only friend I had left was missing. Absent, I told myself. He's just absent. He'll be back on Monday.

The door to the school opened again. I looked up, hoping it was Allison, come back to apologize. But it was another girl from the class, sent back for me.

"Lorelei? Hurry, or you'll miss music!"

I jumped up and followed her inside. Music always made things better.

Everyone else was already in the music room, sitting down on plush beanbag chairs.

"Today, we'll begin our study of musical instruments," Ms. Threnody said, and tossed her long hair over one shoulder. "Beginning with this one." She held out a big, velvet bag.

Her voice was strange. It was deeper than any woman's voice I'd ever heard, and rich. She spoke slowly, considering every word she said, picking each one like a fruit that she rolled around on her tongue before she shared it with us. She opened the bag, and out tumbled fourteen smaller jewel-colored velvet bags. "Choose one, but don't open it yet."

All the girls scrambled for the fuchsia and purple ones. I ended up with a brown bag, the deep rich brown of

Andrew's eyes. I gripped it, trying to feel what was inside. It felt long, thin, and hard.

"You may open them now."

I was opening mine before she gave permission, and so I was first to see the instrument.

"A reed pipe?"

I was confused. It wasn't a recorder, or a penny whistle, or anything I had ever seen before at a music store. It was an old-fashioned flute, cut by hand from some sort of reed. Mine was dyed purplish brown and carved with tiny gargoyles. The mouthpiece was the head of a gargoyle with an open mouth right where I was supposed to put my lips to blow.

Creepy, I thought. I'd have to kiss a gargoyle every time I came to music class.

Ms. Threnody's laughter reminded me of the faraway roar of the ocean. "Yes, dear Lorelei. A reed pipe. One of the oldest instruments in the world, played by shepherds and nymphs in the days before history."

She settled her hand on my shoulder. It felt cold and slightly damp. Ick.

"Ms. Morrigan told me you were studying mythology. This instrument would have made the music the Muses sang to."

"Aren't we going to sing?" I dropped my eyes away from

hers. It was hard to look straight at her for long; the colors of gray in her irises kept shifting and swirling. "I love singing."

She leaned down and whispered in my ear. "As do I, Lorelei. But can I tell you a secret?"

I nodded.

Her voice became a tiny snake that curled through my ear and lodged in my brain. "I can't stand the sound of children singing."

My eyes flew open.

"They don't pay me enough to have to listen to that racket all day long."

"But . . . but you're the music teacher, aren't you? Isn't that your job?" Had anyone else heard her? No, they were all busy unwrapping their pipes and showing them off. "You can't be serious."

"Oh, I am," she said. "As serious as the grave." She picked an invisible piece of lint off my shoulder, and blew it away. Her breath smelled like salt.

"But . . . but . . ." I was furious. I wasn't going to be allowed to sing—none of us were? But we were the students. This was supposed to be our school. "Why not?" I bit out, not caring if everyone heard me. "Why can't we sing?"

She straightened up. "Oh, fine, Lorelei. If you must sing us a little solo, go ahead. But quickly. This class isn't your little Carnegie Hall, now, is it?"

The whole class was paying attention now.

I sputtered, angrier than I had ever been with a teacher. She was making it sound like I had begged her for a solo! Making me out to be some sort of show-off. The kids around me started laughing.

Allison raised her hand, waving it until Ms. Threnody noticed. "Ms. Threnody, don't be so hard on Lorelei," she said.

I looked gratefully at Allison. She was trying to help me out; I would have to thank her later. But then she went on, "She's just upset because her boyfriend, Andrew, isn't here today."

I gasped. Did she think that was funny? From their giggling, I could tell the rest of the girls obviously did.

"I see. A boyfriend." Ms. Threnody crossed her arms over her chest. "Lorelei? Is that so?"

I felt my eyes narrow and gritted my teeth to keep the words I was thinking from spilling out. Ignoring Allison, I shook my head once at Ms. Threnody. She uncrossed her arms. "Well, then. You were so anxious to perform. Go ahead."

And then she said the words my mother had hummed to me every night for years, before I'd sung her our special lullaby. I didn't know how she knew those words, but she did. She plucked them out of my brain like a shell from a beach. "Sing, little Lorelei bird. Sing me a special song."

If she hadn't moved away, I would have scratched her eyes out.

"No," I muttered.

But then she stood in front of me, and commanded: "Sing."

I couldn't resist.

"Sleep, baby, sleep. Thy father guards the sheep. Thy mother shakes the dreamland tree, and promises sweet dreams for thee . . ."

My throat still burned from the sand, and I could hardly hold a note for two counts without coughing. The song sounded terrible. It was the German lullaby my mother had taught me years before, and I had never sung it for anyone else. I tried to stop singing, and the effort made my voice squeak and go flat, then sharp. Somehow, she was forcing me to sing. The last words were almost a moan. "Sleep, baby, sleep . . ."

I was sobbing by the end. Ms. Threnody clapped slowly, obviously enjoying my pain. The other kids looked away, the way you do when someone embarrasses herself terribly.

I closed my eyes. Laughter cascaded over me like the slapping of waves on a boat.

"Would you like me to sing another lullaby, class? It might give you a better, ah, appreciation for the form. Lullabies really can be lovely, when sung properly, and by a gifted singer."

My classmates begged her to. She opened her mouth and began.

I had never heard the lullaby she sang, but I knew it somehow. It was in German and, even though I couldn't speak the language, I understood every word.

> Bist du bei mir, geh' ich mit Freuden
> *If you are with me I go with joy*

> zum Sterben und zu meiner Ruh'.
> *to my death and rest.*

> Ach, wie vergnügt wär' so mein Ende
> *Oh how pleasant would be my end*

> es drückten deine lieben schönen Hände
> *if it would be your lovely hands*

> mir die getreuen Augen zu!
> *that would close my eyes!*

It was terrifying. It was glorious. Every note was a pearl, luminous and polished, glowing from the rich warmth of her perfect tone.

It was everything I had ever wanted to hear in a song, the best, most meaningful music that had ever been made. As she sang, I began to cry; all of us did. The other students were moving toward her, iron filings drawn to a magnet. I sat on my hands and wept. Her voice was the most beautiful thing I'd ever heard, and it made me ashamed of my own.

The song ended, and the entire class burst into applause. The girls hugged each other and the boys slapped each other on the back.

Ms. Threnody turned to me and nodded. "And that is why you will start with a reed pipe."

I nodded back, but my nod was not agreement. It was challenge.

Lunchtime came quickly, and with it, a discovery: I wasn't hungry. I sat down at the table, aware of Ms. Morrigan's eyes on me. I watched the waiters rushing around, noted the glazed expressions on the faces of all the students. They started eating as soon as their plates arrived, and all conversation stopped. The thin waitress I had seen drinking tea brought me a plate piled high with steak. What was her name? I couldn't remember.

"Thank you, Miss . . . ?"

Her hands shook, and she almost dropped the plate on my lap. She didn't answer, but shot a frightened glance at Ms. Morrigan.

"I'm sorry," I said again, "I can't remember your name. Mine is Lorelei. What's yours?"

Her lips worked as if she was trying to answer. Ms. Morrigan nodded slightly, twitched her fingers in a strange gesture toward her own lips, and the woman took a shaky breath.

"Vasalisa," she murmured, her eyes rolling back in her head like a frightened horse.

"Vasalisa?" I had heard that name before. "There's a picture of a girl named Vasalisa in the hallway. From Romania, I think. Have you seen it?" I peered at her face. "Same eyes, too. Was that you?"

She dropped my plate in front of me, and gravy spattered the purple tablecloth. She backed away, muttering apologies. I glanced down. The food looked delicious, but my stomach churned. All I wanted was something plain. Toast, or some fruit. "Vasalisa?" I called. "Could I please have a piece of toast? Just plain?"

But she had gone.

"Fascinating," Ms. Morrigan said. "You're not hungry again today, Lorelei?"

"Not really," I answered, watching the students around me shovel food into their mouths as fast as they could. It was amazing. We hadn't been here a whole week, and it looked like some of them had gained ten pounds. Why wasn't I hungry? What had changed since yesterday?

And then it came rushing back to me in a flood of memory. The science experiment—the sand. The bone sand. I had eaten a handful of it, and now I wasn't hungry, not like before. Why not? Was it . . . magical, like Ms. Threnody's music, and the endlessly full candy bowls? It was the only explanation I could come up with that fit. But it made no sense, unless what I feared—about Andrew—was true.

Were we being fed? Or fattened up?

I looked over at Ms. Morrigan. She wasn't smiling.

"Well, I'm afraid you'll not be much use to me, then," she said quietly, setting her spoon down. I glanced at her bowl. It was filled with some sort of weak broth, no meat or vegetables in it that I could see. She stood up and settled her napkin in her chair. "I'll have to decide what to do with you. Stay here."

I sat wondering what I had done. Vasalisa came back with refills for the other students. None of them had even noticed Ms. Morrigan leaving, and they didn't notice

Vasalisa, either. They just kept eating, eating, eating. I snapped my fingers in front of the eyes of the boy next to me, but he didn't even blink.

"You should eat." The sudden voice right next to my ear frightened me, and I jumped.

"Oh, Vasalisa. It's just you." I shrugged. "I know I should eat. But I don't want to."

"Shh. They'll hear."

I assumed she meant the other wait staff; the students were in no danger of hearing anything. Were the other kids all hypnotized?

"Why are you not eating?" she asked, her eyes darting to the door, then to the tables around us. "Every child feels the hunger. Are you fighting it?"

"Fighting what?" I asked. What had she meant? "The hunger?" I tried, when she didn't answer. She nodded once. "No. Not anymore," I whispered, just loud enough to be heard over the clink of silverware. "I'm really not hungry. Well, I'm a little hungry. Normal hunger. For toast."

"Oh, yes," she said, setting down a plate in front of me. It was toast, but swimming in butter. "I apologize; it is not plain. But we are not allowed to make the plain food."

"Where are you from, Vasalisa? How did you come to work here?" I lowered my voice even more. Fear flashed across her face.

"I, too, fought the hunger." A pause. "I should have eaten. It would have been better. At least then, there is an end."

Before I could ask her what she meant, she practically sprinted for the door. I saw why, a few seconds later, as Ms. Morrigan came back into the room.

"Principal Trapp wants to speak with you," she said.

I followed her out of the cafeteria. No one watched me go, except Vasalisa, who was frozen by the door to the kitchen, her dark brown eyes liquid with pain. For me? I wasn't sure.

Principal Trapp wasn't in her office. She was in my classroom, standing by my desk. When we walked in, I saw what she was holding, and I blushed. It was the myth I'd been working on. I hadn't gotten very far since Andrew had disappeared. *Been sent home,* I reminded myself. I didn't know for sure where he was.

The principal was reading the last part of the story, but looked up when we walked in. The last few paragraphs were a mess, I knew—full of misspellings, sentence fragments, and who knew what else. I wanted to run away from the sympathy in Principal Trapp's eyes, but Ms. Morrigan had her hand on my shoulder, and I had a feeling she would love an excuse to grab me tight enough to leave a mark.

"Lorelei?" The principal's voice was kind, as always. "Alva tells me you're not feeling well."

"I'm well," I said, feeling Ms. Morrigan's nails bite into my shoulder the tiniest bit at the lie. "I'm just not hungry is all. Is that a problem?"

"I'm afraid it is, but only because it worries me. Your energy's been so low, I haven't seen you running in the hallway since the first day." She laughed, and her eyes sparkled as she hinted at our race down the halls. "I thought it might be because of what that unfortunate boy did on the playground."

She looked out the window at the playground, where the sand glinted white as ever, then turned back, her green eyes full of sympathy. "But Alva tells me you're not eating. And that your schoolwork is suffering these past two days." She glanced down at the paper again. "I can't even read most of this, Lorelei."

I wanted to explain that my work wasn't suffering because I was protein-deficient, or whatever she thought, but because my study partner had been absent. But I didn't say anything. I didn't want Ms. Morrigan to know I wasn't up to the work she was giving out. She would use that against me somehow.

"It's her attitude," Ms. Morrigan said. "And aptitude as well."

"Alva, come now. Lorelei's got such gifts—"

Ms. Morrigan laughed abruptly, an ugly sound. "I haven't seen them."

"I know," the principal said. "You've been overwhelmed with work. What if I come in and observe? Maybe another set of eyes—"

Ms. Morrigan interrupted. "With your schedule? You're already doing the job of three administrators. I told you before: I can handle the kids and the cafeteria. You don't need to worry about a thing."

"I'm worried about you, too, Alva. You've got dark circles under your eyes."

"To match yours."

They both laughed. I let out a sigh. They were ignoring me, pretty much. Maybe we were done.

"Can I go now? I promise I'll work harder tomorrow." I tried to step away from Ms. Morrigan—her fingers were pressing against a nerve—but I couldn't. I looked over my shoulder, and into her eyes.

"Not yet," Ms. Morrigan said. "We haven't finished our discussion about your work. And your attitude."

I couldn't breathe. I felt the blue of her eyes like frost on my skin. For a moment, my whole world was pain, fire inside my body, and outside. The searing pain of being burned from the inside out, and held motionless while it happened. I tried to scream, but my lips were held immobile. I was trapped, dying.

That's right, a voice said over the silent screaming. *Pain if you resist, pain if you fight. Pain if you remember. The kind of pain no child has ever known*, the voice mocked, *suffering beyond what any child could endure.*

But the voice was wrong. I had felt a deeper pain, one that had lasted for over a year: the pain of knowing I had done something unforgivably evil.

She promised pain if I remembered? I prayed every day for some way to forget my pain.

"Lorelei?" The principal was waiting for something. She shuffled the papers in her hand, and I realized there was no pain, no voice. Just Ms. Morrigan's cold, questioning eyes, and her fingers on my shoulder. I'd been daydreaming again. Carried away by my imagination. *Focus, Lorelei.* What had the principal been talking about? Oh, yes. My work suffering.

She wanted me to tell her what was wrong, but I just shrugged. I wouldn't say anything in front of Ms. Morrigan, no matter if it got me in trouble.

Instead of being mad, though, the principal smiled and nodded cheerfully, as if I'd done something wonderful.

"Excellent," she said, standing up and dusting her hands off. "You have such potential, Lorelei. I know it. In fact, you may turn out to be the best student I've ever had. But take care of yourself, please? Eat your meals. Let us care for you . . ." She took a step toward me, and Ms. Morrigan's fingers tightened until my shoulder burned with agony. I opened my mouth to scream, but no sound came out. The whole world tilted on its axis, and everything went dark. I fell into a dream, or a faint, but I thought I heard Ms. Morrigan's voice as my eyes closed.

"She's nothing special."

And then, softer, "I think she is."

Chapter 13:
Toil and Trouble

I woke up with the taste of sand in my mouth, and a rock where my heart had been. Was it Friday? I looked at the clock. Five o'clock. So, still Thursday, I thought.

I was missing half a day. It was gone, like a lost tooth. My mind kept searching for those hours, but thinking about them brought a stabbing pain in between my eyes.

Had I hit my head? Did I have amnesia? No, that was way too soap opera. Maybe I was going crazy.

The phone rang, but I didn't bother to pick it up. There was something I needed to remember. Something bad.

What had happened at school? All of my memories from after lunchtime were gone, wiped as clean as Molly's vanity mirror.

The phone stopped ringing, and a few seconds later I heard a shout. Molly's voice sounded far away and echoey. "Lorelei? It's a girl. And when you get off the phone, for the last time, set the table!"

Someone was calling me? No one called me. I didn't have any friends, not anymore. My head pounded when I moved toward the phone. What had happened at school?

"Hello?"

"Lore, it's Ally," I heard. I waited until I heard the click of Molly putting down the receiver before I answered.

"Hi, Ally. What's up?" Why was she calling? Especially after what she had said in music about me. My cheeks burned. *Why can't I forget the public humiliation of Ms. Threnody's class, instead of the after-lunch part*, I wondered. Whatever happened then couldn't have been worse than music, could it?

A lance of pain shot through my forehead as I reached for the memory again.

"I just wanted to call and say I'm sorry," Allison answered. Her voice sounded rough. Had she been crying? "I wasn't myself."

"You mean, in music class?" I hesitated. "What do you mean, you weren't yourself?"

"I don't know," Allison said after a few seconds. "It was

like, I was just filled with . . . meanness. Like I couldn't control it. You know?"

"No, not really," I said. This was her idea of an apology? The line buzzed between us.

"Principal Trapp heard about what I said in music," she said softly. "She called me to her office to talk to me about it."

"Oh," I said. Now I got it. She was calling because she had to. Only I didn't get it. Why was the principal interested? Allison had just made a joke at my expense. Sure, a pretty mean one. But usually, principals didn't get involved in little things like that.

Maybe it was because I had been hurt. Maybe it was because she really does love me.

Maybe I'm special, to her. My heart raced. "What did she say?" I asked.

"She said she wanted Splendid to be a safe place for all her students," Allison said. "And she had zero tolerance for teasing." She paused. "So, um, I just wanted to say I'm sorry. Do you forgive me?"

I didn't answer. She hadn't just been mean once; she'd done it a lot of times. And left me to spend my summer alone, after she'd found out my secret.

"Please, Lore," Allison asked again. "I swear I won't say anything about Andrew Fortner again."

Andrew! That was it. "Okay, Allison. I forgive you. On

one condition," I said, when she started to bubble her thanks. "Tell me something, will you? This afternoon. I can't seem to remember what happened. After lunch."

"You mean, after snack?" Allison sounded amused. "I can understand why everything went fuzzy—you practically ate yourself into a sugar coma! I mean, come on, Lore. I know it's all-you-can-eat candy, but you must have eaten six bowls of Skittles during the social studies video."

"I ate snack?"

"Um, yeah. Although 'inhale' might be more accurate. Oh, wait a minute." I heard a shouted "In a minute, Mom, I'm on the phone," and then Allison was back. "Hey, I have to go to dinner. I'm starving."

"Wait," I said, "Do you mean I was in class after lunch? I came back to class?"

"Um, yeah," Allison said. "You were acting all weird, but I thought that was because you were mad at me. Hey, you're not still, are you?"

"Not?" I asked. Not what? Acting all weird? I didn't know what she meant by that. Since I couldn't remember any of it, I didn't know what to say.

What I did remember from that morning was bad enough. Andrew was missing. I wanted to ask Allison about him, whether she knew where he lived, but I stopped myself. I might forgive her, but I didn't think I could trust her. Who knew when she would get "uncontrollably mean" again?

Allison's voice came across the line, quieter. "Um, not still mad at me. You said you forgave me."

"I do," I said just as softly, and said goodbye. It felt strange, like I was saying goodbye to more than a conversation.

Maybe I could forgive Allison, but I knew if I didn't try to find out what had happened to Andrew, I would never forgive myself.

But that evening, riding all over the neighborhood on Bryan's skateboard, I couldn't find Andrew's house. Instead, I found myself heading for the school, again and again, like every street in our neighborhood led toward it. When I finally got home, it was almost ten, and Molly was on a tear.

The next morning, Molly was still yelling at me. "Lorelei, look at you. Just look at you! What kind of a girl does that to herself?" I glanced down. So I still had a little road rash on my knees. Well, maybe more than a little. It was pretty gross. I picked a tiny piece of gravel away from one of the scabs. I really had to learn how to use Bryan's skateboard, or I was going to need skin grafts.

Who really needs all their skin? Ms. Morrigan's first words to me floated into my mind, interrupting Molly's catalogue of my faults as a girl, stepdaughter, and overall human. If I was right about Ms. Morrigan, if what I imagined was true . . . No. *Crazy thoughts, Lorelei.* I had to stop thinking about it.

I felt like I really was going crazy, and Molly's early-morning yelling didn't help. I crossed my fingers behind my back and apologized, promising never to go off without helping set the table first, promising never to fall off a skateboard again, never to bleed again.

I guess I overdid it. She got even madder, but when I went outside, she didn't follow.

I sat down on the front step, waiting for Bryan to come downstairs, trying to figure out what I couldn't remember. Dad's van was already gone. I needed someone to talk to. I hadn't had anyone since Mom who really listened.

Maybe . . . I turned the thought over in my mind like a fallen leaf. Maybe I could talk to Principal Trapp. She was the only adult who seemed like she really cared about me. Of course, she had said I didn't need to tell my secrets to anyone. But what if I told them—just to her? Not all of my secrets. But I could tell her about my dysgraphia, or whatever it was. Then, if that went well, I could ask about Andrew, make sure he was okay. Who knows—maybe he would be back today.

I stood up. Maybe I could get to the principal during breakfast. If I hurried.

I took a few steps, then broke into a jog. The scabs on my knees pulled with each step, but I ignored them. Dad would probably have a fit when he saw them, too. I could almost hear him now. "Whatever happened to Barbies and pink stuff? Where'd my little girl go, Lore-lore?" He'd said it a hundred times in the past year.

I'd wear pink every day if I could have Dad back, I thought. *If I could have my family back.* I rounded the corner and saw Principal Trapp standing outside the school, waving to me as though she'd been waiting for me all her life.

"Hi, Lorelei the Golden," she called out when I got close enough to hear. "Did you sleep well?"

"Fantastic!" I shouted back, and ran toward her. This was my chance!

But then, the automatic doors opened up and Ms. Threnody and Ms. Morrigan stepped out.

The morning sun slid behind a cloud, and three cars pulled through the driveway, hiding the teachers and the principal from sight. When the cars drove off, they had all gone inside. I had a feeling it was going to be a very bad day.

I had no idea.

During lunch—another meal where no one spoke, and everyone except me ate enough to choke a horse—Ms. Morrigan stood up.

"That was your last chance, Lorelei," she said over the sounds of silverware and chewing. "Stubborn, stupid little thing. Follow me. It's time to clean out your desk."

"Why?" I asked, looking for someone, anyone. The principal? Vasalisa? There was no one there but the hypnotized kids. "Am I in trouble?"

"Oh, I'd say you were trouble itself. But we'll find something to keep you out of the way. A girl as . . . special . . . as you? I know just the place."

I thought she was going to put me in detention. But, as it turned out, they didn't have detention at Splendid.

CHAPTER 14:

The Unspoken Rule

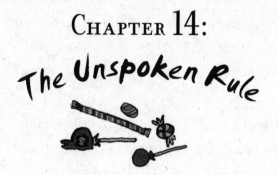

That night, when Dad got home, I ran out to the drive-way to meet him. I was crying so hard that by the time he opened the van door, I could hardly speak.

"Dad. Dad, I have to talk to you." I grabbed his arms, my rough hands catching on the smooth cotton of his shirt. My palms were red and raw from the afternoon's work.

"Whoa, Lorelei. Calm down! What happened?" He put his hands on my shoulders and looked into my face. "Home stuff or school stuff?"

I took a deep breath. "School stuff," I managed. He held me close, rubbing my back the way he used to do when I was little.

After a few minutes, I stopped crying. "Thanks—hic!—Dad," I hiccupped, and we both laughed. He leaned back against the door of the van, pulling me next to him.

"It wasn't that kid Bryan was talking about, was it? Andrew something or other? He didn't come back to school today, did he?"

"No," I said, trying to stay calm, but I couldn't. Hearing his name brought the whole horrible afternoon rushing back. "Dad, it's not Andrew. In fact, that's part of the problem. I think Andrew is dead. Murdered."

"What?" Dad stood up. "Lorelei, is this just more of the same kind of drama you've been coming up with since Molly?"

"Dad! I don't care about Molly. She didn't even want me to tell you. I need you to pay attention."

He stepped away. Great. I'd ticked him off. "Don't care about Molly? I think we'd better have this discussion inside. Is she home?"

"Yes," I mumbled. "She's going to be mad I said anything. I tried to tell her what happened—I mean, she asked me why I was so upset, right? But she thinks I made it all up. She even took the phone away when I tried to call his parents!"

"Well, I'll admit, it's a little far-fetched," he said, pulling on my ponytail softly. "I think I would have heard something, on the news even, if one of your classmates had been murdered."

He wasn't listening to me. I had to get his attention, and I knew one way to do that for sure. One word. "Not if they didn't find his"—I swallowed hard—"his bones yet."

I had broken the unspoken rule.

Dad stopped, his hand trembling on the doorknob. "What exactly do you think happened, Lorelei?"

I knew he probably wouldn't believe me, but I had to tell him what I suspected. "I think my teacher, Ms. Morrigan—and maybe the other teachers, I don't know for sure. They all seem suspicious," I took another deep breath. "I think she ate him."

Watching Dad laugh at me, I remembered why I never told him anything. Why kids didn't tell adults anything, most of the time. Adults don't listen. They don't pay attention, and they don't care.

Of course, Dad hadn't listened to anything I'd said since the day Mom went into the hospital and never came out.

That had been all my fault.

I supposed I deserved to be ignored now.

After dinner, Bryan disappeared into the living room to play video games. Molly went into their bedroom with a magazine, leaving Dad and me alone so that Dad could—in her words—"straighten me out."

I'd shown him my hands. The skin was pink and peeling, and the pads of all my fingers had scrape marks on them.

"How do you explain this, if I'm lying?" I asked as calmly as I could.

"That skateboard again," Dad said and sighed for the tenth time. "Molly said you went out after school for hours yesterday. I wish you wouldn't disappear like that. It worries her."

"Worries her?" My jaw dropped. Molly had only worried that I wouldn't get home in time to set the table.

"She's not the only one worried, baby," he began, rubbing the bridge of his nose with one hand. "Let me just see if I got this straight. You honestly believe your teacher—-and maybe the entire teaching staff at your new school—is fattening up the students to eat them. You think they ate your little friend. And this afternoon, Ms. Morrigan pulled you out of class and put you to work in the kitchens, scrubbing pots. So that road rash you showed me is supposed to be dishpan hands. Did I get that right?"

"Yes," I said. My face felt hot. Even I knew it sounded ridiculous. He didn't believe me. Why would he? It was something from a horror movie, a bad one. All I knew was I had to try. "I don't think the whole staff is in on it. The wait staff seems normal, compared to the others. I haven't ever seen the teachers for the other grades. But my teacher, Ms. Morrigan, and the music teacher, Ms. Threnody? She has to be in on it."

"Of course, I suppose Principal Trapp is in on it, too." Dad sounded tired.

"No," I said slowly. "I don't think she knows there's anything going on. She's really nice. Maybe . . . maybe I need to tell her."

That was sounding better and better. I could already tell Dad wasn't going to help me. Maybe the principal would, if I could find some way to show her what was going on, some way so she would believe me. If I could get her alone.

"Tell her what?" Dad asked. "What exactly would it be that you would say to the principal of your school, Lorelei?"

"Well . . ." I paused. "I think maybe they're . . . witches, or something?"

"Of course!" Dad slapped his palm against his head. "I should have thought of that myself. Of course, there would need to be—what?—three of them. Because there are always three witches around the spell pot, right? But if there *were* three, and they snacked on children, that would definitely point to magic."

He'd figured it out? I nodded, wondering where he was going with this. For a minute, his eyes shone with the same brokenness they'd held for the past year and a half. But then he shook his head in disgust. "For crying out loud. You've got bigger problems than worrying about magic, Lorelei. Real problems. You need to focus on your schoolwork, and try to keep up. This charter school could be a real chance for you to make up for lost opportunities. Get some one-on-one tutoring to help with your problem. You're going to want to get into college someday—"

"College?" I couldn't believe it. He hadn't heard a word I'd said. "I may not live through the week! Did you miss the whole 'eaten by witches' part of this conversation?"

"This isn't a conversation. This is a fairy tale. I always told your mother to stop filling your head with all those wild fantasies. Witches, ogres, unicorns. It's no wonder you can't tell the difference between reality and fiction. If she—"

"Leave Mom out of this," I yelled. My chair fell over as I stood up. "She would have believed me."

"She wouldn't have encouraged this kind of nonsense."

I heard Molly's voice from the bedroom call out, "You tell her, hon!"

"Lorelei, I'm going to call a psychiatrist in the morning. You need help—"

"I need you to listen!"

"I've listened long enough. You have an overactive imagination—always have—but now it's gone too far. Molly was right. I've overindulged you. I let you have your way for so long, you've taken advantage of me and Molly—"

"Molly? It's always about her, isn't it? She doesn't care about me as much as her . . . her pedicure, Dad. Mom would have listened to me. She would have cared. You don't. If you did, you wouldn't have forgotten about her and married that hag. I hate her. And I hate you!"

I couldn't see through my tears, but I felt Dad's hand on my arm, pulling me down the hallway to my room.

"You have no right to say such things about me or Molly, Lorelei. I'm disappointed in you." He looked down at me like I was something stuck to his shoe. "You can come out when you're ready to apologize." He shut the door, leaving me alone in my room, muffling his voice. "I can't believe you would act this way."

"Believe it," I shouted back at him through the door. "Or don't believe it. It doesn't matter. By this time next week, I'll probably be dead. And Bryan, too!"

I heard his footsteps stop, and I said something I shouldn't have.

"Then you'll have what you want. Your old family gone, so you can start over with her."

I thought he was going to come back. I thought he would open my door, I could apologize, and he would listen. But, instead, I heard Molly's voice.

"Do you see? This is what happens when you're too lenient with kids. She's taking terrible advantage of you—and me. I can't tell you how hard she's been on me. But, really, babe. A psychiatrist? They're so expensive. Maybe the school has a counselor . . ." Her voice trailed off, and their footsteps moved away.

I stayed in my room through dinner, and most of the weekend. I came out to read the Sunday paper, though, to see if there was a missing person's story about Andrew. Nothing. Of course, I was grounded, and Molly gave me the evil eye anytime I went near the phone—not that I knew Andrew's phone number.

On Sunday evening, Molly and Dad called a family meeting to let Bryan and me know that they were signing us up for an optional after-school sports program at Splendid "to help Molly out since we'd been so hard on her," according to Dad. "She needs time to adjust to a new life. Some time to herself. You kids need to be more understanding. Especially you, Lorelei." It sounded like Molly had written a script for him; he kept looking at her after every sentence, making sure he got his lines right.

I needed to be more understanding? I had a very bad feeling that I understood far more than I wanted to about a whole lot of things. But, of course, I had that wrong, too.

CHAPTER 15:
Stepmothers

On Monday morning, I slept in—thanks to Molly not talking to me, which, as it turned out, even included *not waking me up*—and missed school breakfast. Bryan had gone earlier, and Molly didn't trust me not to run away between the house and the school, obviously, so she drove me there. In silence.

I went to class, but my desk wasn't there. Andrew's desk was, though.

And to my complete amazement, so was Andrew.

"Lorelei?" he whispered. He looked as surprised as I felt.

"Andrew? I thought you were—"

"Lorelei Robinson?" Ms. Morrigan was standing there,

right by my elbow. "I'm sorry, you must have forgotten your class transfer."

"Class transfer?" What was she talking about?

Ms. Morrigan's eyes gleamed as she pitched her voice so the whole class would hear. "Yes, dear. Your special class. For children who have special needs? Because of your problems with writing?" She shook her head. "Your test scores place you somewhere around the second or third grade for basic writing proficiency. I'm not sure how you were ever promoted to sixth grade. Negligent teachers in those underfunded public schools, I suppose. But we'll take care of you here at Splendid." She pushed me gently toward the door. "You may go to the special workstation I set up for you. Hurry up, now! You have a lot of work to do today, and your tutors are ready to help you learn everything a girl like you can."

"Special workstation?"

"Yes," she answered, her mouth twitching with laughter. "The one you went to on Friday afternoon?"

Oh. I got it. The kitchen.

"Oh, Lorelei," I heard Allison whisper. She wasn't looking at me, wouldn't look at me. She was embarrassed she knew me. "How awful," she said.

"You have no idea," I answered.

My face was on fire. The whole class was silent, except

for Neil Ogden, who whispered "moron" as I walked past him. There wasn't time to say anything to Andrew. I would have to speak to him later. At lunch, maybe.

The hallways were silent and empty. That was weird. Usually there were a couple of kids in the halls, dodging whatever part of class they disliked most, or just messing around. Where were they all today? Too full from breakfast to run around anymore? I thought back to Friday, to my ideas about Ms. Morrigan and the food. I had been so certain of what had happened to Andrew—but now he'd come back to school. Maybe I was wrong about a lot of things. Maybe Andrew had been wrong too, about the sand.

Something tickled the back of my neck. I swatted at it, thinking it was a mosquito, but there was nothing there. Then I realized: There was something. I had just passed the pictures of the other Splendid schools. I stepped back to look at them. I wanted to see if the little girl Vasalisa really did look like the one who worked in the kitchen.

She did. Her face was still curved into that hideous frozen smile, the one that had the word *run!* hidden just behind the teeth. She wanted to warn me, I thought.

"Warn me of what?" I whispered. "Ms. Morrigan? Is she really a witch?"

I waited, but there was no answer, just the feeling of

hundreds of eyes following me as I walked on. I sped up; that hallway was really creeping me out.

I turned the corner too fast, though, and almost ran into Principal Trapp, who was walking toward me, her hand on the knob of the teacher's workroom door. I glimpsed just past her arm a gleam of copper. The kettledrum? It had been moved, and it didn't look exactly like a drum now. I craned my neck to see. The principal shut the door and looked at me, surprised and disappointed, like I'd done something wrong.

"Lorelei? What are you doing in the hall?" She raised one perfect, dark eyebrow. "Didn't you hear the announcement at breakfast? Hallway privileges have been rescinded for the duration of the week . . . oh, yes. You missed breakfast today, didn't you? Do you have an explanation for that?" Her eyes widened. "You weren't feeling ill, were you?"

I shook my head. "My stepmom," I said. "I'm getting the silent treatment. She won't even say 'Get out of bed' to me."

"That's terrible! You must be joking."

"I wish. Stepmoms stink."

Principal Trapp laughed, and the whole hallway seemed lighter. My chest seemed lighter, too, like there was hope for me, even with a teacher like Ms. Morrigan. Principal Trapp wasn't my friend, but she was one of those adults who got kids. She really cared; it was there every time she looked at me.

"Don't tell anyone, Lorelei," she said, "but I have a little secret."

"What?" Secrets in Splendid? This had to be good.

"*I'm* a stepmother," she said.

"Really? Who's the lucky stepkid?"

"You know her pretty well already," she teased, "even though she may not be your favorite person right now. I hear she sent you to detention on Friday for something or other. And she told me this morning she's signed you up for special tutoring to help with your academic problems. I know it's not fun, but we want to help you, Lorelei. You are so important to us here at Splendid. I know I feel that way anyway."

I wanted to melt at her praise, but I was too busy being horrified.

"Ms. Morrigan's your stepdaughter?" There went my plans to tell her how evil my teacher was being. How had a woman as nice as the principal ended up with a daughter that monstrous? "I didn't even know you were married."

Her face fell. She looked so sad that I knew something terrible had happened. She leaned back against the wall, as if she couldn't hold her own weight anymore.

"He passed on many years ago. Only a day after our wedding, actually. I had so little time with him. But he gave me the most wonderful thing I could ever imagine: his daughter."

"You really love Ms. Morrigan, don't you?" I said, my heart plummeting. It was just like Dad with Molly. They couldn't see the witch right in front of them.

There was no way I could tell the principal about her stepdaughter. "You love her . . . like a mom."

She nodded.

"Molly isn't that way," I said. That was an understatement.

"No," she said. "She lacks that maternal spark, doesn't she? I hate to say I noticed that right away." Principal Trapp leaned over and cupped my chin in her hand. "If you were my stepdaughter, Lorelei, I would take better care of you."

My eyes prickled. Why couldn't I have Principal Trapp for my stepmom? Oh, yeah. Because Dad had already married the useless Molly. I didn't say anything; I thought I might say what I was feeling, and that wouldn't make me sound very nice. So I kept my lips tight shut. But she looked like she could tell what I was thinking as she stroked my hair. It had been over a year since anyone had done that.

"I wish," I said at last. "I wish you could."

Principal Trapp hummed tunelessly. "I'll tell you another

secret, dear Lorelei. You're special. The last time I met a little girl like you, I had to marry her daddy so I could be her mother." She pushed a stray piece of hair behind my ear, and I shivered. "You remind me very much of her at this age. Stubborn, strong-willed, beautiful—with those same golden curls. But so unsure of herself, as you are. She really needed someone to help her find her calling."

As a witch? I thought, but then I knew what she meant. "She really loves teaching, then."

"She loves children," Principal Trapp corrected, and straightened up, patting her hair back into the bun. "She cannot get enough of them. I've never seen anyone who cared so much, even feeding them herself to make sure they grow up big and strong."

"Yeah, she's practically stuffing us full of knowledge," I mumbled, "and cake."

This was it. My moment to say something, if I was going to say anything at all, about the weird way Ms. Morrigan obsessed about the students' mealtimes. Maybe I should just point out how eating all that junk food wasn't really good for you?

"You know, about the meals. They're not very, um, balanced . . ."

The corners of her mouth lifted. I guess it was weird, to have a kid complaining about too much junk food. I was about to tell her it wasn't the type of food, but the quantity, when the door to the workroom swung open.

Ms. Threnody had been inside listening, I assumed, the whole time.

"Oh, it's the little singing girl," she trilled. "Have you been practicing your reed flute?"

I tried not to glower at her, but I couldn't help it. "No. I left it at school over the weekend."

"And this is the girl you were so certain would be my star pupil, my dear principal?" Ms. Threnody shrugged. "I will keep trying with her." She glided toward us, and I looked away from her hypnotic eyes.

I glanced down at a slight movement. Her fingers were trembling—the way Ms. Morrigan's had a few days before. The bones and veins on the backs of her hands protruded so much now, it looked grotesque. Had she lost even more weight? She looked skeletal. Weak.

The principal's voice interrupted my thoughts. "I'm sure you will, although not today. Lorelei has special tutoring now," Principal Trapp said and, smiling, warned me to hurry up. "Alva told me she'd set up something unique, and knowing how much she loves children, it'll be unbelievable. I'll want to hear all about it. So, hurry!"

"Yes," Ms. Threnody said, shaking her hair down over her face. "No dawdling. You have so much work to do today." Her shoulders shook. Laughing at me. I wanted to smack her in the face with my fist. She raised one eyebrow. *Just try it*, she whispered into my mind, her lips not moving at all.

Had I imagined it? I didn't think my imagination was that good. Frightened, I practically ran down the hall toward the cafeteria. With every step, I doubted myself more. She couldn't be a witch. Principal Trapp had said she'd known her for years. But if she wasn't a witch, she was still one of the meanest people I'd ever met. Next to Ms. Morrigan.

How had Ms. Threnody and Ms. Morrigan both fooled the principal for so long?

I'd heard the expression that love was blind. I'd seen it in action with my dad and Molly. But this was worse than that. Did love make you a fool, too? Maybe they'd found some way to keep Principal Trapp in the dark, to hide their meanness from her.

Or maybe she's so kind she can't see the darkness in them, any more than she sees the darkness in me.

Maybe this was all a terrible nightmare. No, my nightmares weren't this horrible. It had gotten so that the worst my sleeping mind could come up with wasn't a patch on what was really happening to me during the daytime.

The cafeteria kitchen was busy with the sounds of pans

clanging and water running, but when I walked in, everything stopped. A dozen thin faces took me apart with their sharp eyes. Then, as abruptly as they had stopped work, they started again. No time to waste.

Vasalisa approached me. "You're back?" she asked. She was speaking more clearly now, even though she still had an accent. "Why?"

"Why not?"

She looked horrified. "You told your parents, yes? What the Morrigan made you do on Friday. They saw your hands. Why would they send you back?"

I could have told her the truth—that my dad thought I was making it all up, or that I was crazy, that he hadn't listened to anything I said since Mom fell—but I didn't. What if I was wrong? Maybe I had made it all up, imagined it into something far worse than it was. Vasalisa seemed okay, but I didn't know what she'd say if I told her I thought my teacher was a witch, so I just answered, "Because I'm a kid, and no one ever listens to kids."

"True," she said, and handed me a pot scrubber. "But you could have run away. You should have. Washing dishes is the least of the punishments she has devised."

I was surprised she was even talking to me. On Friday, I had spent three hours scrubbing the kitchen fixtures, and the staff had treated me like I was a spy. They'd given the term "silent treatment" new meaning, even if it seemed sometimes they couldn't have spoken if they'd wanted to. "Where would I go?" I asked.

She didn't answer.

I turned to the sink that was full of breakfast dishes and started running hot water over the grease-covered skillets, scrubbing until Vasalisa came to take over. I guess I wasn't scrubbing fast enough, but it was hard. I was too short to really reach into the sinks.

"Too slow," she said, and handed me a towel. "Dry."

Those three words were the only ones spoken aloud for the rest of the morning. Every time I started to say anything, one of the kitchen crew shushed me. There were at least a dozen of them, mostly young men, but three girls like Vasalisa, too. They were all silent and scarily thin, but no one snuck a single bite of food the whole morning. And the food smelled heavenly. I hadn't eaten breakfast, so I was starving hungry.

Gustav—or Otto, I couldn't remember which was which—set an enormous platter piled high with spaghetti in front of me while he went back to get a gravy boat full of marinara sauce. The steam from the pasta dampened my face, and I inhaled. Vasalisa was grating fresh Parmesan cheese on the stainless steel counter behind me, and the nearest men were chopping what looked like large hams into paper-thin slices. No one was looking. I took a noodle—just one, and sucked it in.

"No!" Someone had seen.

Vasalisa turned white, and her lips opened and closed, like a fish on a bank. "We can't eat!"

A few seconds later, the door to the kitchen slammed open, and the quiet grew thick, heavy, and ominous—the atmosphere before a tornado. Colder, too, I thought, and shivered as I swallowed. Colder?

It was Ms. Morrigan.

"A little mouse is nibbling at our feast," she hissed. "Who is it?" She made that strange motion with her fingers close to her lips, and said three words. "You may speak."

I swallowed quickly.

No one answered. No one even looked at her, I noticed. I dropped my eyes, too. It was hard not to look up, when her footsteps rang on the white tile floor, closer and closer to me. The footsteps stopped, right in front of me.

One noodle. How had she known?

Magic, my inner voice insisted. *It has to be magic.*

"It couldn't have been you, dear little Lorelei. Not after what I told you on Friday. Surely," she said, and reached down with one hand to pull my chin up, "you listened to my instructions. What did I tell you?" Her fingers were icicles, and her breath was rank, like rotting meat.

"You told me to clean," I said at last. "And not to come out of the kitchen unless you told me to."

"And what else?"

"And not t-t-to eat," I stuttered. "But I have to eat something!"

Vasalisa made a tiny, birdlike sound. "Ah!"

"Oh, you want to eat? How remiss of me. My apologies, dear. I'm sure I can get you something," Ms. Morrigan said. "We don't want anything to go to waste, now do we? Yes, I'll make you a plate. Of course, you'll have to eat every bite before you can go home today."

She slid past me, toward the workstation in the back of the kitchen where two of the men had been shelling crabs all morning for Tuesday's crab cakes. I rubbed at the places on my chin where her nails had scratched me and watched

as she heaped a plate full of crab shells. She dropped the dish down on the counter in front of me.

"There you go. Your lunch. You eat it all up now. As soon as the last bit is gone—oh, and believe me, I'll know if a single claw is left uneaten—you may go home."

She left the room before I started to cry. Vasalisa wrapped her arms around me, and rocked me until my heart felt as wrung out as a dishtowel. My tears soaked her apron, and after a while I realized the top of my head was wet. She had been crying, too.

"Why, Vasalisa?" I asked, but she just shushed me, and rocked back and forth. The rest of the kitchen staff ignored us. Lunch was coming, and they had work to do.

Me? I had shells to eat. And I couldn't go home until they were gone. The thought made my stomach heave, and I knew I had never been this alone.

Then I heard the cracking sound right next to me.

"Vasalisa? What are you doing?" I watched through swollen eyes as she picked up the smallest crab shell on the plate and stuffed it into her mouth. She chewed over a hundred times, her teeth sounding like she was eating glass. I winced as she swallowed. "Stop!" I said, and grabbed her hand when she reached for another crab leg.

"No, let me," she said. "I can do this for you."

I let my hand fall, my mind spinning, and watched her

eat three more crab shells. She took a break to drink some water, and I asked, as softly as I could, "Why?"

I didn't need to say any more; she understood. She swallowed, rubbed her throat, and whispered back, "I had a sister. Liliya. She was your age when I was taken. When we were both taken."

"Taken?"

"By the witch."

She meant Ms. Morrigan. Maybe I'd been right all along. "Where is your sister now?"

"Gone."

"Gone?" It took me a moment to realize she meant dead.

"For many years now." She took another drink, and coughed. "I was unkind to her. Selfish and vain. I called her terrible names and made her feel very bad."

"Sounds normal to me," I said. "I don't have a single friend who's nice to her siblings."

"It is not normal in my country," she said, shaking her head. "There we take care of our families. I did not. I chased her into the forest near our home, telling her I would kill her if she stole my wooden doll again." She stopped talking long enough to choke back a sob. "I sent her into the arms of the witch. When I followed, too late, the evil one took me as well, but made me her slave. I was too thin, she said, to make even a snack."

"A snack?" I smiled weakly, but stopped when I saw she wasn't joking.

"There are many kinds of witches. This one is, at least, not wasteful," Vasalisa replied, and picked up another small crab shell. She sucked out a small piece of meat that clung to the inside of the claw. "And I have eaten worse."

"Worse than this?" I couldn't help it: My voice rose and cracked. "Worse than crab shells? You can't be serious."

A dark-haired, tall boy rushed past us, carrying an empty tray. "Keep her quiet, or La Llorona will be back in here with death for us all." He stopped when he saw what Vasalisa was doing, and made a face. "Here," he said, taking the plate of crab shells from her and dumping them into a pot on the stove. "You boil them first, with vinegar. They get soft, they are easier to chew. Women!"

Vasalisa stuck her tongue out at his back—the first time I'd seen her look even vaguely playful since we'd met—and dragged a stool over to the stove so I could stir the shells while she washed dishes.

"What did he call her? La Llorona?"

Vasalisa shrugged. "There are a thousand names for her. Antonio comes from Mexico. She is the ghost witch in their children's stories. It doesn't matter what you call her. Better not to speak of her at all." She laughed, a dry sound she obviously hadn't made much. "The Morrigan told us all to speak when you tasted her food, but forgot to command our silence when she left. It is . . . rare for us to be able to converse. We must not draw attention to her mistake. No more talking for now."

"But I need you to tell me what she's done," I insisted. "I have to know. I mean, I'll admit I suspected Ms. Morrigan was a witch. And maybe she is. But that doesn't matter. Somehow, I have to get to Principal Trapp and let her see what's going on here—the way she treats you, us. Me. It doesn't matter if it's magic or not. It's abuse, plain and simple. If she can actually see what's happening to me, she'll make Ms. Morrigan let me go . . ." I stopped.

The kitchen had fallen silent again, and everyone was staring at me as if I'd sprouted a horn.

"What?" I said, when I saw Vasalisa's face change from horror to pity. "I meant, she'd let all of us go. Not just me."

"You don't even know, do you?"

"Know what?" I wanted to disappear. But why should I be embarrassed? What did they know that I didn't? "That my teacher is a witch, probably? You said it yourself."

Vasalisa waved the others back to their work, and lifted her hands as she spoke. Her skin was rough and chapped from dishwater and scouring pads. "You believe the witch to be the Morrigan?"

"Yes, Ms. Morrigan," I said softly, wondering why she

was asking this. They had to know—she was keeping them here, wasn't she? "And I think Ms. Threnody might be one, too. But I'm not sure about that. I've only met her two times."

"Twice more than enough. Yes, the Rusalka, she is also one of the evil ones. But there are three, little one. Always three."

"Three?"

"Do American parents not tell the tales anymore? Do they leave their children ignorant as well as defenseless?" She turned her head down and to the side, like she was thinking of spitting. "They guard their homes full of plastic but leave their true treasure to be plundered by the wicked."

"What are you trying to tell me, Vasalisa?" I glanced at the door. I could hear the classes running past the cafeteria on the way to recess. Ms. Morrigan would be outside, making sure they all ate their snacks. If I hurried, I would have time to run to the office and tell Principal Trapp about the kitchens before lunch. Show her the crab shells! That would do it.

But a soft voice stopped me. "The Morrigan is only the stepdaughter of the witch," Vasalisa whispered, her voice trembling. "She and Threnody are witches, yes. But their leader, their stepmother—the true witch—is the one you call Principal Trapp."

CHAPTER 16:
In the Soup

I refused to believe it. Principal Trapp as the head witch? They had to be wrong. I was one hundred percent certain it was Ms. Morrigan.

I didn't say it out loud, but some of them must have been able to tell I wasn't convinced. Gustav, for one, spent the next hour slicing garlic bread and salamis and telling me the stories of how Principal Trapp kidnapped him and his brother, Otto, from their home in Austria.

"We had a third brother," he murmured, "named Nicholas, with the voice of an angel. But Threnody grew jealous, and they sacrificed him to her envy eight years past this October."

I didn't ask what he meant by "sacrificed him to her envy." I had a bad feeling I knew.

Gustav told dozens of horrible stories about Principal Trapp, and the ways she had captured children all over the world.

"The worst was when she built her school next to the favelas of Rio de Janeiro," Gustav whispered, his eyes full of dark memories. "Some parents there knew what she was, but they sent their children to the school to die anyway. 'Better to die with a full stomach in a witch's mansion, than from hunger in a shack made from cardboard and wire,' they said. They were wrong. There is nothing worse than what she has planned for her students."

I didn't ask what she had planned; I couldn't. Gustav seemed to think the students at Splendid were being fattened up for a feast. I wanted to tell him that I had thought that too, but Andrew had come back. He hadn't been eaten. But I could tell Gustav believed it. It all made sense, if what he said was true: the enormous quantities of food, the mandatory meals and snacks all day long, and the trance that came over the students whenever they came into contact with food.

Vasalisa spent her time in the back of the kitchen convincing the wait staff that I wasn't a spy sent by the principal.

Some of them were eyeing the knives and me in turn, and I was grateful for her help.

I *needed* help. But I couldn't trust any of them, not really. And they were too scared to draw attention to themselves, not that I blamed them after hearing Gustav's gory tales of what had happened to the few brave, foolish kitchen workers who had resisted in the past.

Then I remembered. There was one person who might be able to help me.

Andrew.

Lunchtime was drawing closer. Vasalisa was tracing swan designs on the edges of the crème brûlée dessert plates with fruit puree. The designs were beautiful—Vasalisa could have been an artist if she hadn't been captured and forced to work in the kitchen. I waited until she was done, then touched her sleeve. She backed away, then asked what I wanted.

"There's a boy out there who can help us. The boy who was making me eat the . . . the sand. He knows something's going on. He could help. "

"Who?" She faked a smile, like I was a child telling a wild story, and she was humoring me.

"His name is Andrew."

"Oh, no." Her smile vanished. "The fat boy? Tell me he is

not your friend. Stop thinking of him now, little bird. It will hurt less if you do."

"Hurt less? What are you talking about?"

Her dark eyes shone with tears again. "He is to be eaten in two days. Gustav has already been sent to prepare the soup pot."

"The soup pot?"

"Yes, in the teacher's room. We do not have any pots large enough to boil a child." She paused. "Not whole."

My mind raced. The teacher's room? Then I understood. The copper gleam—the kettledrum.

I shook my head. "But Ms. Morrigan doesn't eat them. I thought that," I explained when Vasalisa looked at me as if I'd lost my mind, "when she took him to the office. But he was back at school today."

"She didn't eat him last week," Vasalisa explained slowly, "because the ceremony was not prepared. But now the wood has been chopped, the pot filled. He will be the first sacrifice since he is the largest. I am sorry to tell you this."

"W-why?" I cleared my throat. "Why would he be eaten?"

"The bone broth is almost gone, and all of the witches' magic will fade soon."

"Bone broth?" I was so confused. What was she talking about?

With a quick glance at the door, she stopped washing and pulled me to the back of the room. In the corner, a squat, black cast-iron stove sat with a lidded copper pot on one of its burners. Vasalisa picked up a metal hook from next to the stove, and used it to take the lid off the pot.

The pot was almost empty, but at the very bottom, I could see some small pieces of bone moving in the simmering water. The bones were small and bright white, each one no longer than a child's finger.

A child's finger? *Your imagination's running away with you, Lorelei. Focus.*

"What . . . what is it?" I asked, when I could breathe again.

Vasalisa took a ladle full of water from the plastic bucket at her feet and splashed more water into the pot. The steam rose up around my face and I breathed in.

For a moment, it smelled like the noodle soup my mom had always cooked for me when I was sick. Then the smell changed, overpowering me. If grief had a scent, it was coming from the pot in front of me. Something fell into the broth, and I realized I was crying. I stuffed a fist into my mouth, and backed away. Vasalisa dropped the lid back on, looking worried.

"It is what they eat," she whispered. "What they have

always eaten to restore their magic. Broth made of the bones of children. They eat the meat first, and then the strong stock. When that is gone, they boil each bone until every whisper of magic has been leached away. When the bones turn bright white, the magic is gone. These are the last of the bones from the school in Brazil. And this broth is now almost too weak to fuel their spells."

CHAPTER 17:

A Message in Code

The best part of nightmares is the waking up. You find yourself in your own bed, with your favorite pillow under your head, the familiar sounds of your house at night all around you. I found myself wishing for my old nightmares—the monster under the bed, the man in black at my window, the ghosts that slid under my door—instead of this new one that would not let me wake up.

I sat on a stool, trying not to hyperventilate. Vasalisa sat next to me. "You are well?" she asked. Black spots danced before my eyes, but I took a slow breath and asked the question before I could lose my nerve. "They eat children? For real?" She nodded once. "Why?"

Her eyes fluttered shut. "Maybe long ago they ate

magical creatures. I have heard them tell stories of unicorns and manticores. They might be legends, or lies. In these times at least, children are the only magic the world has to offer. But they must eat many to grow stronger. They adore America, with its neighborhoods full of well-fed children, its parents who trust strangers as long as they call themselves teachers."

"But I'm not even a kid! I'm eleven, almost twelve. And my brother, Bryan? He's thirteen already, and huge. Nobody would call him a kid."

She just shook her head. "Were you enticed by the playground? Was your brother attracted to it?"

I nodded, remembering how we had both reacted to the sight of all the new equipment.

"Then you are children. Only children would be drawn to it. You may not call yourselves such in this country, but you are still children nonetheless. And food for the witch."

She walked back to the front of the kitchen, stopping to stir the softening crab shells as she passed. She handed me the dishtowel again, and went back to washing the dozens of plates that were piling up next to the sink.

Lunch must be half over, I thought, with the small part of my brain left that could think. My thoughts felt cloudy, dreamlike. Could it all be my imagination? Could it all be a dream, a horror I had stitched together from threads of guilt and sadness? I pinched myself, hard enough to make red crescents rise up on my arm, but the nightmare didn't end.

"I need to get out there," I whispered to Vasalisa a few minutes later. "I have to warn him."

"Impossible. The Morrigan watches very closely at meal-time. Servers are not allowed to speak at all, and never to the children, not that it would do any good to try. The children fall under the spell of the food. They would not hear us if we shouted in their ears."

"Andrew would," I replied. "He doesn't eat like the others. He can control himself."

Vasalisa just shook her head.

"Too dangerous. And if they see he is not eating, they will kill him that much sooner, before he grows too thin. Your friend is lost to you, Lorelei. Best not to think of him. Think instead of a way to get your parents to listen to you. You must not return tomorrow."

I put a hand on her arm. "I need to get a message to Andrew. A note. A piece of paper, maybe, on his plate. He'll see it."

"The witches would know if anything came from the kitchen that was not food," she scoffed. "There is no way to send this message, unless you can write a letter with mashed potatoes and butter."

"*That's it!*"

I spent the next few minutes trying to write with mango puree on the side of a fresh plate of crème brûlée. I couldn't put much there, and it had to be in code. A place to meet, a time, my name. That was all.

"You cannot put your name," Gustav said, sighing, and wiped the letters from the small plate. "She'll kill you outright when she sees it. And me as well."

He had agreed to carry the dessert out, but only after Vasalisa had asked for me. I could see why he had agreed, looking at her blush as she smiled at him. She wasn't beautiful, of course; it was impossible to be as malnourished as she was and stay attractive. But her eyelashes were thick and dark, and her eyes so large in her narrow face, I could tell she had been pretty once. As I watched her fish another crab shell out of the pot on the stove and chew the softboiled piece without complaining, I realized she was still beautiful, in a way that would never fade.

She reminded me of my mother, I thought, watching her work to swallow again. Near the end, Mom had been thin like that, too, and swallowing had hurt. Everything had hurt; even the touch of the sheets on her skin. But she had called me up onto her hospital bed when she saw my tears, folded her arms around me, singing our lullaby until I had cried out. Her arms had been every bit as thin as Vasalisa's, and her eyes just as beautiful.

"It's okay, Gustav," I said. I grabbed another plate. "I won't write my name. Not exactly."

I reached into the pot, took out a crab shell, and placed it in my mouth as I wrote slowly, saying each letter out loud as I went, on the edge of the dish. Some letters were bigger than they should be, some smaller, but I got them all down: PERSEPHONE @ OPEN FLAME. Then I placed two pomegranate seeds at the bottom of the plate.

I hoped he would get it. I hoped he would see it. I hoped against hope that he would come, and listen to my story, and believe me.

I forced the crab shell past the lump in my throat, and reached into the pot for another one. I had to finish them all and sneak out before two o'clock.

Chapter 18:
The Secret of the Sand

The kitchen staff helped. I don't know why I expected them to stop me. Maybe because I knew, and they knew, that their lives were at stake if the witches caught them doing it. Still, they helped me eat the shells and told me the best way to get to the science wing without being seen.

"Won't she know?" I asked, swallowing the last shell. It didn't taste all that bad, to tell the truth. The water had softened it down to rubber, and Vasalisa had smothered it in lemon and melted butter left over from the lunch plates. But the idea of eating shells still made me choke. "She has to have some sort of detection system or something."

"She did, once. But in this school, with her magic so

depleted, she has been conserving. Also, the children have been allowed to walk wherever they want until today, yes? So the hallways have no alarms. She has made it easy for you. Now eat." She handed me a chicken leg and some French fries.

"But—we can't," I started to protest, but then saw that the whole staff was picking through the leftovers from lunch, choosing pieces of food that had been left uneaten when lunchtime had ended.

A gruff voice at my elbow startled me. "Scraps for the dogs. It is the only meal we are allowed. Eat quickly." Gustav handed Vasalisa a plate with an untouched pile of mashed potatoes and a veal cutlet with only one bite missing. "Eat, Lisa."

"Thank you," Vasalisa murmured. She was blushing, I noticed, and wouldn't look Gustav in the eye.

She liked him, and from the way Gustav was holding out the plate of food to her, he liked her, too. She took the plate with a trembling hand, and their fingers brushed. When they touched, both of them looked toward the window in the kitchen door.

"I'm sorry," Gustav said softly, his voice horror-filled. "I didn't mean to touch—"

Vasalisa interrupted. "No, it was my fault. If she comes in, I will tell her I was clumsy."

"Maybe her magic no longer works for this," Gustav said, and raised his hand to brush her face, almost. His fingers traced the outline of her cheek, centimeters away.

Of course they weren't allowed to touch, I realized. They weren't allowed to talk. If they talked, they would plan an escape. And if they touched, if they grew that close, they would help each other. Work together. Fall in love. They would become family, and protect one another.

All of the other kitchen workers were suddenly busy with tasks that kept their backs turned to Vasalisa and Gustav, giving them a strange sort of privacy in the middle of the bustle. I couldn't help but stare as Gustav's hand sketched the line of Vasalisa's profile in the air. How terrible would it be to fall in love with someone when you were a prisoner? They had nothing to dream of, nothing to plan for. They were just a few years older than Bryan and me, with their lives before them. Only their lives would be filled with backbreaking labor and silence, not dates and high school proms. No holding hands, no first kisses. No love, no marriage, no future.

I looked away at last, embarrassed by the longing and pain in their faces. I ate the chicken leg as fast as I could, and pitched the bone into the trash.

"No," Otto said, and picked it out of the container. "The witch does not allow waste. We grind all the bones here."

He fed the bone into a machine that hung on the wall near the back door, and a whirring sound filled the room. I watched as fine sand filtered from the machine and piled up in the bucket on the floor underneath.

"What do you do with it now?" I asked, but I had a feeling I knew.

"We wash it, and then it is for the playground."

"The playground sand is made of chicken bones?" I felt sick, but the thought of the sand being ground-up chicken bones was better than what I'd thought after I had seen the witches' broth. "Ick. I ate a whole handful of that stuff."

"Chicken bones?" Otto answered after a moment. "Only a very small part." He wiped his face. Was he crying? Why would he cry now, over a handful of bone scraps?

Unless . . . .what I had thought was true.

Unless Otto had spent years in kitchens like this, forced by the witches to grind the bones of children into sand. Glittering, white sand that had been drained of every bit of magic, sand that was recycled, remade into a fantasy playground that drew more children near.

To their deaths.

Otto spoke again. "I know now how you were able to fight the hunger."

"You do?" My voice trembled. I didn't think I wanted to hear him say anything else.

"I believe so. The witches' spells are made from the magic of those children. That the bones would try to reclaim what was once theirs seems . . . possible."

I'd been right about the sand after all.

And now the bone sand was inside me, soaking up the addictive magic in the food. My stomach lurched.

He reached out and stopped just short of taking my hand. "I do not want to grind the bones of your friend, or of any child. But when I resisted her before, she found ways to make me do it."

"Ways?" My mind buzzed with horrible possibilities.

He turned his head away, like he couldn't bear to look at me when he spoke. "She tortured my friends. Killed my brother and sister. She visited slow, painful death on all those around me until they begged me to do her will, so their misery could end." He shook his head once. "If it had been my own pain, I would never have done it. But to watch your sister's fingers be taken, one at a time . . ." His voice broke. "I was too weak to bear it. She will find a way to force me to grind children's bones again. Maybe she will use you. Go, now. Warn him."

"Be back by three o'clock," Vasalisa called as I ran for the door. "The witch inspects the kitchens then, and you must not be missing."

I left by the back door. Hugging tight to the wall and

crouching low under all the windows, I moved as quickly as I could toward the science wing, only stopping once to control my breathing. It wouldn't do Andrew any good if I hyperventilated now.

The playground sand—the brilliant white dust that had made me impervious to the hunger—swirled up into a dust devil around me. Now that I knew, I could almost hear voices, hundreds of shouts for *Mother, Mother!* resonating inside my skull.

What can I do? I thought, tasting salt tears and grit in my mouth.

Mother! the sand answered back, stinging my face.

"First, Andrew," I replied.

I opened the door to the science wing and slipped in without anyone noticing me. Or so I thought. I was halfway down the hall when a voice called out, softly. "Lorelei?"

I spun around, my shoes squeaking on the tile. Thank goodness! "Bryan?"

"What are you doing here?" He was walking down the hallway toward the music room. "Skipping class? Weird for you, huh?" He rubbed his stomach.

"I was just going to the bathroom," I lied. "You?"

"Just went," he said, and belched. "Had the runs."

"Yuck, Bryan," I said. "You're so gross."

"Better out than in, right? At least I made some space.

I could use a snack." He continued walking, leaving me there. "Thank goodness they have candy in class. Don't know why I'm so hungry these days. Growth spurt, or something." He hesitated. "I hear you have a boyfriend. That kid who was messing with you. Andrew?"

"He's not my boyfriend," I said, wondering if Allison had been spreading that rumor all over the school.

"Good," Bryan answered. "He's not good enough for you. Hurting you? Even if you are a brat." He took a few more steps down the hall, the moment of brotherly concern past.

"Bryan?" I whispered after him.

He turned his head, and I could see that his neck was thicker and softer than it had ever been. He was getting bigger every day. He was probably the second biggest kid in the school, I realized. If I couldn't save Andrew, Bryan would be next.

"What, squirt?"

"Don't eat too much candy, okay?" I said, knowing how dumb it sounded.

"Jeez, Lorelei. Do I look like I need a mom?"

We both stopped as his words filled the silence around us with memories. "Get back to class," he said after a few seconds, and he stalked back down the hallway toward the eighth-grade classroom. He turned the corner and was gone.

I waited and waited, with no sign of Andrew. I stayed in the science lab for forty-five minutes, crouched behind the door so no one could see me if they walked past the window. I had finally decided to leave when I saw the door-knob turn. The door opened, and Andrew walked in, look-ing confused.

"Lorelei?"

"Shhh!" I hissed.

"What in the world are you doing down there?" He looked thinner than he had on Friday; his cheekbones were starting to show. His hair was sticking out in all direc-tions, as usual, and seeing it made me smile. His messy hair seemed so normal, in the middle of the whole nightmare that my life had become.

"Keep it down," I warned, and motioned him across the room, as far from the door as we could get. We hunkered down behind the lab station, hidden by the enormous stain-less steel table.

"No one knows you came here, right?" I asked first.

"Of course not. I told them I had to go to the bathroom."

"I didn't even know if you would get the message."

"Well, it took me a while to figure out the two seeds meant two o'clock. Thank goodness I read a lot of spy books."

"Why were you so late, then? I only have five minutes before I have to get back."

"Get back where? Where have you been, Lorelei? Ms. Morrigan says you went to a special writing class, but I don't think they even have Special Ed here."

I held up a hand. There wasn't enough time to go into all of it. "Listen, Andrew . . ."

I stopped when he grabbed my hand gently. I blushed. Was he holding hands with me? Maybe Allison had noticed something I hadn't. Did Andrew . . . like me? But then I saw his face; he was horrified.

"Lorelei, what happened to your hand? It's all red and sore looking. Both of them! Has someone been hurting you?"

I thought about telling him about the kitchen, and the crab shells, but I didn't. "No time," I said, and pulled my hand free. "Listen. I don't know if you figured this out or not, but Ms. Morrigan is a witch."

"Yeah, that's a nice word for what she is," he started, but I cut him off again.

"No, Andrew. You were right. She's an actual witch," I said. "Minus the broomstick. You were trying to tell me all along, and I didn't believe you, but I do now. And I know what they're planning."

"Wait. You're telling me our teacher is a witch? A magic-spell, black-cat, wart-on-her-nose, fairy-tale witch?"

"Since when is this news to you, Andrew? You're the one

who figured it out at first. The candy bowls that never get empty? I'm sorry, by the way. She got a hold of me that day in the hall. I was really mean afterward, but it wasn't me, exactly. I'm glad you're okay."

Andrew looked like he'd swallowed a bug. "A witch, Lorelei? Really?"

"Didn't you know? Isn't that why you made me eat the bone sand?"

He slumped back against the stainless steel table leg. "Yeah, I knew they were . . . something. I mean, I figured it was some sort of psychological experiment, you know? Something less crazy. Maybe they were hypnotists, or some sort of cult. That would have been way better."

"What happened after the, um, thing on the playground? After I ate the sand?" Had Ms. Morrigan tortured Andrew? What had she done?

"I got sent home. On the way back home, I told my parents about the bone sand, and they called the principal. She came over to our house and talked to them. After that, they wouldn't listen to anything I said. I figured she'd brainwashed them or something. That's why I thought a cult, you know."

"The principal came over?" I swallowed. Maybe she *was* part of it! I didn't want it to be true, but if she had gone to Andrew's house alone—he interrupted my growing panic.

"Yeah, with Ms. Morrigan."

"Ms. Morrigan was there, too?"

He nodded, and the panic faded.

"I'm pretty sure the principal's under her spell, too. So it was Ms. Morrigan."

"Who did what?"

"Brainwashed your parents, or magicked them, whatever. It means the same thing, Andrew. For us."

"What?" His dark eyes looked as scared as I felt. "What's going to happen?"

"We're going to have to save ourselves. You and I are the only people who can see through her spells, because we ate the sand." I took a deep breath. "And that's not the worst of it."

"How could it get worse?" Andrew was sweating, even in the air conditioning, and he rubbed a hand over his face. "What could be worse than witches with mind control?"

"They're losing their power, Andrew," I said. "Getting weaker. Haven't you seen them shaking? They need to eat something to help fuel their spells."

"They? I thought you said it was just Ms. Morrigan? Are you sure Principal Trapp isn't one, too? I mean, it is her school and all. And could Ms. Morrigan really do this on her own?"

"Ms. Threnody's a witch, too," I told him. "No question now. But not the principal."

"That doesn't make sense."

I sighed. Why wouldn't he believe me? "She hasn't done anything bad to you, has she?"

"No," he said slowly, "but she is the principal. It's her school."

"But she works all the time, so she's not around when they do the worst things, right? And she loves them. Ms. Morrigan," I revealed, "is actually her stepdaughter."

"Then the principal's definitely in on it, Lorelei."

"No," I insisted, "it's like my dad and my stepmother. Molly's evil, too—well, not evil like the witches. But he loves her, so he can't see any of the bad about her. Love is blind. I thought it was just a saying, but it's true. They want love so bad, they can't see what's right in front of them."

He shook his head. "Fine. You said the witches need to refuel. On what?"

"Well, to start with—you."

I don't know what Andrew was going to say because the door to the science lab opened, and Ms. Morrigan's voice called out.

"Hello? Is that you, Andrew? What are you doing?"

Andrew put a finger to his lips and stood up.

"Hi, Ms. Morrigan. I was just looking for something I thought I left in here the other day. I thought it might have rolled behind the sinks."

"Well, you've almost missed afternoon snack. And I told the class this morning, the freedom to roam the hallways has been rescinded for a few days." Her footsteps clicked across the tile and I froze, my heart beating faster with each step. But Andrew stepped toward her, and she stopped.

"Why can't we go where we want, Ms. Morrigan?" he asked. "I mean, we have to ask to go to the bathroom? That doesn't sound like the Splendid Academy we all know and love."

He was joking with her. I had never heard him sound so fake. He laughed. "Did one of the fourth graders get lost in the hall?"

"No," Ms. Morrigan said, and I heard them both move closer to the doors. "We just had some concerns about a few of the bigger boys spending so much time unsupervised. They were taking advantage. But I'm sure that problem will be solved shortly." The door swung open with a swish. "I'll walk you to the playground. Snack is chocolate-covered cashews today!"

"I can't wait!"

The door closed.

I wanted to kick myself. I hadn't told Andrew they were

planning to cook him in two days! I hadn't even given him my phone number or made any sort of plan to meet up, so we could figure out what to do. And now kids weren't even allowed in the halls. How was I going to get back to the kitchen without being spotted?

I looked at the classroom clock and almost fainted. It was 2:57. I had to be back by 3:00!

I ran to the door I'd come in through and peeked outside. Darn it! The playground was teeming with kids, and Ms. Morrigan and Ms. Threnody were both standing off to the side, watching the oldest boys' football game with particular interest. *Probably trying to decide who they're going to eat after Andrew*, I thought. "I hope you choke on a finger bone," I whispered, and turned to face the long, empty hallway behind me.

There was no help for it. I was going to have to walk right past the teachers' workroom and most of the classrooms to get to the cafeteria. I took a deep breath and stepped slowly, trying to look like I had every right to be there. I was just going to the bathroom, I thought, practicing my excuses. Getting a drink of water.

I passed one classroom, then two. The sign outside the next one said EIGHTH GRADE. I saw Bryan's name on the list of fourteen students and dared a quick glance inside. Bryan was sitting at his desk, reading a book and eating candy.

The teacher, writing something on the chalkboard, had her back to me, so I couldn't see her face. I started to move past the window, when she turned her head to say something to a student on her side, and I realized I knew her. It was Ms. Morrigan.

I remembered that girl in the bathroom had said her teacher was a Ms. Morrigan, too, so she must have been in eighth grade. The two teachers had to be sisters, identical twins at that. They looked exactly the same, from the braided blonde hair down to the bright yellow skirt.

Two teachers like Ms. Morrigan? I cringed at the thought. One of her was enough evil for any school.

I walked past and noticed an empty plastic bag on the floor. I picked it up; I never could stand people who littered, but at Splendid all the kids did it. It wasn't like there were any adults around who cared. I looked into the next room, a seventh-grade classroom. There was no teacher in the room, not that I could see, and most of the kids were playing some sort of board game on the rug.

Then Ms. Morrigan stepped out.

"I thought I saw you here, Lorelei," she said, her mouth twisting into what might have been a smile. "How did you leave the kitchens?"

"How-how . . .?" I couldn't make the words come out. I had just seen Ms. Morrigan on the playground, and then another woman who looked just like her. Either she was a triplet, or . . . "Are you Ms. Morrigan?"

Both eyebrows flew up. "She told me you were the smart one, you little toad. I told her you were just another sheep. I was right. You don't know anything, do you?"

"I know enough," I said. My mind kept returning to the impossibility at hand. How could she be inside, outside, and in more than one classroom?

Well, duh, Lorelei. Magic. Of course a witch could be in more than one place at a time.

"What do you think you know?"

"I know you're a—" I stopped, realizing that if she thought I knew she was a witch, my life would be over faster than I could blink.

She grabbed my arm and shook me. "What do you think I am?"

I spat the words out in the same tone I used when Molly was particularly horrible to me. "I think you're a witch." Only I didn't say *witch*. I used, as my kindergarten teacher would have said, a rhyming word.

Ms. Morrigan's face turned white, and her eyes sparked. I don't think she was used to being called that. "Who helped you? You're not clever enough to have gotten out unnoticed without some help."

"No one," I said. Inspiration struck, and I held up the bag in my hand. "We finished the dishes early, and I knew I wasn't supposed to just sit around. So I left. I'm picking up trash." She stopped shaking me and looked in the bag. There was a used tissue inside. "I started in the cafeteria, and then worked my way down the hall."

"How very industrious of you." Her eyes narrowed. "Get back to the cafeteria. Our new after-school program starts in an hour, and the children will be coming in for an after-school snack."

"Another snack? But they're eating snack right now."

If they kept feeding them this much, the whole school would be ready to cook before Friday.

Ms. Morrigan leaned down and pinched my cheek, hard. Her sharp-edged nails cut into the skin as she pressed them deeper. I tried not to cry out; she'd like that. It didn't hurt any worse than road rash, I thought, as she squeezed. No worse than falling out of a tree. I felt something warm trickle down my cheek. Blood.

Ms. Morrigan pulled her hand away and licked the blood from her fingertips. "You're not very perceptive, are you? Nothing special at all. I don't know what she sees in you." I didn't speak, couldn't. If I made a sound, I would cry.

"No," she said. "You're stupid and worthless. Just a girl who won't eat."

She turned away, and I ran.

When I got back to the cafeteria, the kitchen staff was standing against the wall, stricken looks on their faces. Vasalisa was crumpled in a chair, weeping silently.

And Gustav was gone.

CHAPTER 19:
The Nature of Their Power

I knew without asking that the witch had been there.

"She came for Gustav right after you left," Otto whispered to me over the dozens of plated chocolate cashew clusters. No one looked toward the back of the kitchen, but everyone was aware of Vasalisa crumpled in the corner by the door, next to the bucket of sand. "She knew they had touched, and she made them choose which one would go. Gustav spoke first." Otto's voice broke. "He spoke his own name, and she took him."

"Where . . . where is he now?" A terrible thought occurred to me. "Is she going to eat him?"

"No," Otto answered quickly. "Not one the age of Gustav.

He is no longer a child. There would be no magic to gain. He will become one of her watchers."

"Watchers?" I didn't understand.

"Yes. She could not make him into one of her kind. He was a good man. And no witch has magic enough to change a soul." Otto hesitated and looked toward the back door. "He has become a tree, maybe, or one of the mounds of earth bordering the property."

"She'll bury him?" I asked, trying to wrap my mind around it. "By the playground?"

"No," Otto explained slowly. "She has the power to transform with her magic. To create. She does not waste anything she can change. She will make him into something else. Something that cannot run away or fight her. Or love."

"How do we stop her?" I asked, and Otto stopped just short of covering my mouth with his hand.

"No! Do not speak of such things. There is no way. She is too powerful."

"But there's only one of her." I paused, remembering the hallway. "I think. Anyway, there are lots of us. None of us are fooled by her magic. And her magic's getting weaker, right? Can't we overpower her?"

"We cannot even overpower the weakest—Threnody." His eyes looked as bleak as a winter sky. "They keep us half-starved, too weak for any real resistance. How would we have the strength to overcome the principal?"

"Wait," I said. "You're telling me . . . the *principal* was here? She came in and took Gustav herself? Are you sure it wasn't Ms. Morrigan? I just figured something out. Ms. Morrigan can be in more than one place at a time."

"No, she can only make you think that," one of the other girls said, looking up from the tiny, sugar-crusted viola blossoms she was setting down on the plates next to each cashew cluster. "The Morrigan has power over the mind. Threnody has power over the voice. And the principal has power over everything she sees."

"Enough," Otto interrupted. "The principal was here."

"Ms. Morrigan can make you think things, right? Maybe she just made you think it was the principal!" I paused. "It can't be the principal. She's not evil. She's always been kind to me. Loving. Like a . . . like a mom."

Vasalisa raised her tearful face. "You make excuses for her? I told you, I saw her kill my sister. She made me grind her bones into sand myself, made me scatter them on the ground. My own sister! Is your mother a witch, then? A devourer of children?"

"My mother is dead," I shot back. "I don't have a mother."

"And the witch would be a good substitute?" Her face

twisted in disgust. "Was your mother such a horrible person that you would replace her memory with a killer of innocents like the principal?"

"Vasalisa?" A soft voice came from the door. "What . . . what are you saying about me?"

It was Principal Trapp. She looked utterly stricken, tears falling silently to the pristine, white tile floor. "And what is Lorelei *doing* in here?"

CHAPTER 20:
Perfectly Named

"'A killer of innocents'?" Principal Trapp whispered as we left the cafeteria. She leaned against me as we walked, her weight making my shoulder ache. In the hallway, she rested against the wall, took a deep breath—or tried to—and swiped her arm across her face. "But what she said doesn't matter. The only thing I'm concerned about right now is you. What was happening in there, Lorelei?"

We stood right outside the cafeteria. I could see Vasalisa through the window in the cafeteria door. She was watching me, but it didn't matter. I put my hand out and patted the principal's shoulder.

Vasalisa's eyes narrowed. I had become the enemy, her expression said. I was in the company of the witch.

I didn't care what she thought. She was wrong, anyway. They all were. Principal Trapp was clearly innocent.

"It doesn't matter," I said. "Just . . . you . . . you didn't know I was in there, then? Working in the kitchen?"

"How could you think that?" Her red-rimmed green eyes stared into mine, and I saw despair, horror—concern—in their depths. "How could anyone—" She broke off with a short, harsh laugh. "Of course, what should you think? I'm the principal. This is my school. Everything that happens here is my responsibility, isn't it?" She held a hand out to me tentatively, like she was afraid I might slap it away. "So I am at fault. I wouldn't blame you if you never spoke to me again. Never trusted me."

It was too much. The hurt in her eyes called out to me. *I'd* felt that way before: that no one would ever trust me again. That I was to blame.

I still felt it.

I couldn't do that to her. "No," I said, "I don't blame you."

I looked back over my shoulder right before the principal enfolded me in her arms. Vasalisa was gone.

I closed my eyes and tried to ignore the principal's perfume, the smell of lilies that inevitably reminded me of the cold, quiet funeral home where I'd seen my mother's body for the last time. The principal was still crying softly, and I found myself singing a lullaby with no words, notes strung together, to calm her, the way my mother had for me.

After a minute, she straightened and wiped her eyes. "That's beautiful," she said. "You have a gift."

"Ms. Threnody didn't think so," I said cautiously. Was now the time to tell her about Ms. Threnody? Warn her about both the witches?

Would she believe me, now that she had seen what her stepdaughter had done to me?

"Then she was wrong," the principal said. A tear slipped silently down her pale cheek. "Perfectly named, my little Lorelei."

"You know the story?" I asked. I usually didn't bring it up. It was sort of creepy.

"Of course I do. Lorelei, the mermaid on the Rhine who sings so sweetly, sailors dash their ships on the rocks just for the chance to hear her before they die?"

"That's a nice way to put it," I said. "She killed herself and became a witch. She killed those sailors."

"They were drawn to her. There's a difference. And she traded her old life for a better one, for eternal life." She stroked my hair again. "I knew from the first time I heard your name that you would be special. I was drawn to you." She held out her hand. "Now let's get you cleaned up."

I walked down the hall with Principal Trapp's arm around my shoulder, my heart light for the first time in days. There was no way she could have faked those tears, that pain.

She hadn't known. She really hadn't known I was working in the kitchen. So it was possible—in fact, I was sure it was true!—that she didn't know about the other terrible things that were happening. My heart felt so light, I thought I might float away. I leaned into her arm. I felt safe, and warm, and loved.

When we got to the front office, she sat beside me, her hands in mine softer than the velvet upholstery of the sofa. "How could Alva have done such a thing?" I closed my eyes and let the silver waterfall of her voice cover me, refresh me. "How could she have thought I would allow it? You know I never meant you to be sent to the kitchens"—her voice broke—"don't you?"

I nodded, and raised my hand to cover hers on my cheek. "Thank you," she whispered, and I could hear relief in her tone. "You're safe now, with me. Did you have lunch?"

"A little," I said, remembering the hastily swallowed chicken. Remembering, as I thought of that frenzied lunchtime, the others who had been there with me. Who had helped me. I opened my eyes a crack. The lines around Principal Trapp's mouth still spoke of pain and embarrassment.

"I'll get you something to eat. Something sweet," she said.

"The other kitchen workers," I began. "You didn't know how she treats them? How she hurts—" I stopped, watching a silver tear roll down her face, followed by another.

"You think I knew about that?"

"No," I reassured her, "I know you didn't." Another tear rolled down her cheek and splashed on the dark green velvet, leaving a jagged stain. "We can talk about it later," I said. "You look tired."

"I'm sick," she said. "So very, very sick."

My heart pounded. Was she sick like my mom had been? Was she dying, too? I forced myself to ask the question, though the words tried to stay unsaid, leaving a bitter taste on my tongue. "What kind of sick?"

"Sick at heart," she said, her eyes meeting mine. "Nothing more. Sick at what happened to you today." She fought for a smile, roughly wiping a tear away. "When I was little, my mother would tell me stories when I felt sick or sad."

"Mine did, too," I said, feeling the familiar ache in my heart as the memory of my mother surfaced. I pushed the pain aside.

"Would you tell me a story, Lorelei?" she asked. Her green eyes, so like my mother's, shone with unshed tears and something else. Compassion? "Tell me a true story."

I knew what she was asking. She wanted the story of my mother's death. I tried not to flinch. She couldn't understand how much it hurt me to even think about it, or she wouldn't have asked. I closed my eyes, wondering where to start. Wondering if I could.

The memory started where it always did—the day Mom fell. I'd been harassing her to go out, to take me somewhere, even though she was exhausted. She'd begged me to let her rest. *I'm not feeling well, Lorelei,* she'd said. *Let's just talk. I could read you a story?* But I'd thrown a tantrum and insisted. She had promised to spend the day with me, promised to do whatever I wanted, I reminded her. *Let's go, Mom. The movie's starting in five minutes.* I pulled hard on her arm, harder than I needed to, angry that she was tired again. She was always tired, always sleeping or resting. Her foot caught in the rug, and she fell toward me. Her legs hit mine, bruising me, but something worse happened then. Two sounds, like sticks wrapped in wet towels, breaking, a liquid shattering. "My legs!" she cried out. I looked; her bones had pierced the skin of her calves. White bone, flecked with red blood. She screamed until they took her to the hospital.

My fault.

My family's secret.

The splinters of shame I'd carried with me since that moment edged closer to my heart, like they did each time I relived that day. I edged away from the memory, afraid that the splinters would wound me even more deeply.

I felt damp fingers on my cheek and opened my eyes. I'd been weeping. Principal Trapp sat next to me, her fingers tangled in my hair, a large splinter resting on her lap.

A splinter? No. A stick.

"Thank you for telling me, Lorelei," she said. My heart stuttered. Telling her? I hadn't said a word. Had I? I licked my lips. They were dry.

Bone dry.

"I . . . I didn't say anything."

"You didn't have to, my darling." A tear trembled on her eyelid; her face flashed dark and bright. "I know everything that is in you. Everything that is so much like me. So much pain and darkness. So beautiful." She tapped the stick against her lips, once, twice. It shone white and silver as it touched her mouth, then changed back to a plain branch when she lowered it. *Magic*, I thought.

It was no stick. It was a wand.

I closed my eyes again.

Vasalisa had told me the truth about the principal.

Andrew had been right.

I had been wrong. Dead wrong. And now I was in her arms. Worse—somehow, she was in my mind.

I knew I should run, fight. I tried not to think of such things. How much could she sense? How many of my thoughts could she read?

Enough, it seemed. "Fight me? You . . . you don't want to hurt me, do you, Lorelei?" My scalp tingled as she stroked my hair hesitantly. "Like you hurt your mother?"

I felt a tearing inside, like the splinters I'd carried for so long had finally reached my heart and begun to kill me, too. Could I hurt her, the only one to show me love since Mom?

My heart twisted. "No," I whispered. "Of course not."

"Will you be my daughter, then? I'm so lonely, Lorelei."

My mind was spinning. "You have . . . her," I said, meaning Ms. Morrigan.

"She's not you, my darling. She's not capable of the things you can do."

"What things?" I asked. I really, truly didn't want to know.

"You fought the hunger and won," she crooned. "They all do that, all my servants. Alva, Threnody. But you . . . you did more. A child, with magic so strong you could not be fooled. You discovered our secrets, didn't you?"

"Some of them," I admitted, my voice shaking.

"And you have your own secret. One as dark as any of

mine. A very important one." I opened my eyes again and saw she was smiling, eyes shining. "She'll never be able to take my place, because she didn't do what you did. What I did. It has to start that way, you see, or else you can never have the full power, no matter how much you eat."

What we did.

I knew what she meant. I had killed my mother.

But no one, except my brother, had ever said the words out loud. In fact, everyone other than Bryan had said I hadn't done it. I couldn't have done it, couldn't have known.

I was just a child.

She must have been sick for months, hiding it so we wouldn't worry. The cancer had already spread through her body, making her bones brittle.

The broken legs would have happened, sooner or later. A fall in the kitchen in the night. A stumble on the stairs.

It could have happened any number of ways. I wasn't to feel guilty. I wasn't to blame myself, the doctors said, the neighbors said.

And with every word, they had made me understand that I *had* done it, but it was shameful, a secret.

I was never to speak of it, my father had said. Never to tell a soul. And, except for Allison, I hadn't.

"You killed your mother, Lorelei. Just as I killed mine.

Power, you see? It's the oldest way to take power, and so few children these days have done it, can do it. I knew, when I met you—when I learned your secret—that you would be my new daughter. And here you are." She stroked my hair again, and I fought the bile that rose in my throat.

"I've been looking for a girl just like you for so long."

CHAPTER 21:

One Night To Decide

I knew what I had to say. I just couldn't get the words to come out. The thought of calling her "mother" stabbed at my heart worse than the pain I'd lived with for a year, and my lips refused to open.

I figured if I told her no straight off, though, I wouldn't have long to live. Or at least she would keep such a close eye on me, I wouldn't have the chance to warn Andrew about the soup pot. My head buzzed with caution.

"You see it, you must. That bond between us. Our shared nature," she crooned. "Don't you, Lorelei? My new, best daughter."

I fought back a scream, holding my breath to do so.

When I realized she was holding her breath, too, I tried to nod, but her fingers had tangled in my hair.

"Don't you?" she repeated. Her voice was a discordant bell ringing, warning me to answer.

"I . . . I don't know. It's all so much to take in." I tried not to breathe too quickly, but I knew she could feel my heart beating hummingbird fast. I closed my eyes and slumped against her, feigning exhaustion. "I'm so tired. I need to sleep."

She didn't buy it, I could see. But she brushed her hands, helped me up, and led me to the door. "You've been working too hard," she said, stroking my hair again, wrapping her fingers around one of the curly pieces by my face. "Anyone can see that. Rest tonight. Clear your head. You're a clever girl; I know you'll see clearly in the morning. Make the right decision, Lorelei. By tomorrow morning, we'll both know if you'll be my protégé, or . . ."

She didn't continue. *A tree?* I wondered. *Or a mound of dirt?*

Or an appetizer?

I wasn't positive I had what it took to say no. A dark part of me wondered if I really wanted to say no at all, but I thought about Vasalisa. I wouldn't do that to her.

That evening, I couldn't eat, couldn't speak, not that Molly or Dad noticed. They made their lovey-dovey faces at each other over dinner, not even looking up when I pushed my chair back and carried my plate to the sink.

Bryan noticed, though.

"What's up now, Lolo?" He hadn't called me that in years, and the strangeness of hearing the nickname made me look up.

I couldn't tell him about Principal Trapp. He wouldn't believe me. But I could ask him a question, the question that had been plaguing me all day. "Bryan," I asked, "do you think I'm evil?"

"Um, what?" He half-smiled, thinking I was kidding. "There you go again, imagining crazy stuff. Of course you're evil. I've been telling you that for years. Stupid, too." He crossed the floor to the doorway.

"No, seriously," I said, scraping my plate into the sink. I watched the peas, the instant mashed potatoes, and the fish sticks—Molly's gourmet cooking—slide down the drain. "Do you think, maybe, a person who did what I did . . . becomes evil? I mean, once you do something really bad, does it change you, somehow? Permanently? So other people can tell?"

He didn't answer.

I waited two, three, four seconds, and looked up.

He wasn't even in the room anymore. I could see him through the open doorway, setting up his gaming system.

He pointed the video game controller at the television screen, clicking the buttons fiercely.

I knew it didn't matter what he thought. It only mattered what the principal thought.

I slipped out the kitchen door, grabbed Bryan's skateboard from the corner of the garage, and jumped on. I was still grounded, but I didn't think anyone would notice; I could hear another television blaring inside Molly and Dad's room.

I had to think.

The neighborhood was dark, except for pools of light around the street lamps. It was dumb to be skating at night, but I figured the worst that could happen is I would get hit by a car and die. Something a lot worse could happen at my school—probably was going to happen the next day, unless I agreed to turn to the dark side.

The cool breeze blew through my hair, and I sped up, pushing off from the asphalt like I might leave the ground, fly. If I just kept going, I could run away. I wouldn't have to deal with any of this stuff. I could get picked up by the cops, maybe tell them my parents were abusing me, so they wouldn't take me home. It seemed like the perfect plan for about ten seconds, until I realized that meant Andrew wouldn't have anyone to help him avoid the soup pot.

I had to come up with a plan. What did I have, though? A head witch who thought I was especially evil and capable of being a super-witch myself. Not a positive, in my book. One friend who knew mostly what was going on. A few people in the kitchen who didn't trust me, but would do anything they could to help me trick the witch.

My stomach growled, trying to get its two cents in. I was hungry, since I hadn't eaten.

I had a resistance to magic. Surely that would help somehow? But I got that from eating the sand, not from anything I did.

A thought tickled the back of my brain, but I couldn't quite tell what it was. I'd reached the drainage ditch at the far edge of the playground, though, and something else caught my attention. The ditch was full of water, even though it hadn't rained in weeks. Weird.

I looked past the ditch to the mounds of earth that shielded the school from sight. There was a new mound, just as the kitchen staff had said. A new pile of dirt. I squinted, trying to make out what I was seeing. Ignoring the whisper of the leaves that stirred around me like sleeping snakes, I picked up the skateboard and walked across the grass.

I leaned down near the mound and felt the ground. It was damp. More than damp, it was seeping water. Maybe a sprinkler head had broken off, or a pipe had burst underground. *Probably a burst pipe*, I thought, wishing that were what I really thought it was.

Because the water, when I touched my fingers to my lips, was salty. It tasted like tears, like the mound was weeping, enough tears to fill the ditch. I backed away and slipped on the lip of the ditch. *Yesssss*, the leaves whispered. *Tearssss* . . .

I scrambled against the slope, but dropped the skateboard. It rolled down and disappeared under the black water. The wind stopped, and I thought I heard a door inside the school open.

I ran all the way home, my heart pounding so hard it felt like it would burst.

CHAPTER 22:
Witch Material

That night, I dreamed of my mother. She was dressed in white and she had Vasalisa's dark eyes. The tubes from the hospital snaked down the sleeves of her gown. She didn't speak, but her eyes told me everything I needed to know.

I knew what she thought. I was the one who should have died. I should suffer. Not Gustav, not Otto, not Vasalisa. For what I'd done to her, I should feel pain every day. "I do," I said to her. "Every day."

I tried to move toward her, to hold her up, but I tripped and pulled her down instead. Just like that day over a year before, she screamed, her legs folding under her. The sick, cracking sound of her bones twisting and breaking filled my mind. When I lifted her up, though, it wasn't Mom. It was Principal Trapp, with her green eyes and her flashing face. "I'll be your mother," she said, and reached out to stroke my hair. "A beautiful, golden girl should have a mother like me. It's only right."

I felt her fingers in my hair even after I woke up. I looked at the clock by my bed: 5:00 a.m.

I tiptoed to the kitchen, grabbed the phone and the directory, and slipped outside to call Andrew.

There were seventeen Fortners in the phone book. Twelve of them yelled at me for calling before sunrise, asking for Andrew. I didn't care, I just dialed faster. I didn't have long before Dad would open the garage door and see me hunched down outside. A light came on inside and pooled on the lawn, a sure sign that Dad was in his bathroom. I dialed faster. Andrew's life depended on me not screwing this up. One ring, two, three . . .

"Hello?" A man's sleepy voice on the line.

"Yes, I'm sorry for calling so early. This is Lorelei Robinson. I'm trying to reach Andrew Fortner."

The phone made shuffling noises. I heard a woman complain, "What time is it?" and then a boy's voice.

"Lorelei? What are you calling for? It's not even six." It was him. I took a deep breath, and the words tumbled out.

"Andrew, I don't have long. I need you to know. The

principal is a witch, too. She magicked your parents, and all the other kids in the school. The only reason you and I aren't still eating as much as the others is—"

"The sand," he interrupted. "You said that. But then you said they were going to refuel. What did you mean?"

"Andrew," I whispered, hearing footsteps behind me. "They're fattening up the students to eat them." The line buzzed between us as the words sank in.

"You're not kidding, are you?"

"No, I'm not. They put me to work in the kitchen once they figured out that I knew."

"Are they planning to eat you?" he asked, his voice cracking on the last word. "Don't come to school today, Lorelei. Stay away. I'll help you run away, if your parents won't listen—"

"Andrew," I broke in. "They're not planning to eat me. Principal Trapp's trying to recruit me. Says I'm evil, like her."

"Evil? You're not—"

"Maybe I am. That doesn't matter," I said. The footsteps were closer. "I'm not worried about me. Andrew . . . they're planning to eat you."

The line buzzed again, and then I heard laughter, soft and bitter on the other end.

"Of course they are. I'm the fattest, right? I'd make the perfect meal. Plenty to go around." His words reminded me of what Ms. Morrigan had said on the school tour—there had to be a lot of students, or there wouldn't be enough to go around.

"Andrew, it's you who can't come to school today. Stay home. Lie to your parents; tell them you're sick. The witches' powers are fading, so they have to eat someone soon. Really soon. The kitchen staff says they're planning to eat you tomorrow. They've got the soup pot set up in the lounge—"

The phone was wrenched out of my hand.

"Lorelei?" It was Dad, dressed in his jacket and tie, his expression all business. "Have you forgotten what *grounded* means? And who are you talking to?"

Twenty seconds later, Andrew was off the line, and I was in deep trouble, but I didn't care. I had told him what he needed to know. He would be safe. Now all I had to do was figure out a way to keep my brother out of the soup pot, too.

On the walk to school, Bryan left me behind as usual. "Bryan?" I called out. "Wait up."

He surprised me; as soon as he heard my voice, he pulled out his earbuds and stopped. "What's wrong?" he asked. "You look bad. Worse than yesterday, even."

"Thanks," I said. "Just what every girl wants to hear."

"Well, good thing you're not a girl. You're just my sister," he joked. "Seriously. Your clothes are a mess, your face is cut up, and you have massive circles under your eyes. You're having nightmares again."

"How did you know?" I asked.

"I heard you. I never could sleep when you cried at night, not even when you were a baby." He surprised me then; I felt his warm arm wrap around me. "Don't worry about stuff so much, Lolo. You may be a pain in the butt, but you're my pain in the butt. I'll take care of you, like Dad said. If anyone messes with you, I'll take 'em down."

And then he tried to trip me. I laughed and tripped him back—we'd played this game a thousand times. I was quicker, and sneakier, and he fell a few minutes later, face down on the grass.

"Call 911!" he moaned. "Paramedics!"

"Hospital food for breakfast, coming up," I teased. A thought hit me. Mom had joked that the bone cancer wasn't what hurt the most; it was the hospital chicken. "Practically poison," she'd said.

Bryan hopped up. "Miss school breakfast? No way!" He grabbed his backpack. "Race ya."

Poison. That was it.

A part of me couldn't believe what I was contemplating, but a part of me could. I mean, I was such an evil kid the head witch wanted me for her student. For her *daughter*. Maybe she was right. Maybe I was like her. Because I knew exactly what I was going to do.

I turned back to the house.

"Where are you going?" Bryan called.

"I'm going to get some medicine," I yelled back over my shoulder. "I'm not feeling so well all of a sudden." I ran as fast as I could. I needed to get to the kitchen in time for breakfast.

When I caught back up with Bryan, he was almost at the school. "What's in the backpack, Lolo?" he asked. I shifted it on my back, hearing the faint clicking, like I had packed a pet rattlesnake for show and tell. I didn't know what to say, but it didn't matter. He'd already stuck his earbuds back in. I hoped no one else asked me that question.

"Just poison," I whispered.

Ms. Morrigan met me at the kitchen door. "You're late again." She poked a finger at the scab on my cheek. "Lazy girl."

"Sorry," I muttered, trying not to meet her eyes. My backpack burned against me like it was full of coals. I had never been very good at lying, and I sure as heck didn't want to practice on a witch who wanted me dead. So I kept as still as I could. "What am I supposed to do today?" I asked, trying for meek.

She straightened up, but she breathed heavily doing it,

like it hurt to move. "Your lucky day. I've put you to work making marzipan. Your favorite."

I sniffed the air. I could smell it already, the almond-sweet hint of my favorite dessert in the air. I had to work not to smile. This was perfect. You could hide any taste—or smell—with enough almond extract. "Great," I mumbled.

"Of course, if you decide to try any of it, I'll have to make you another special meal. We're out of crab shells, but I'm sure I can come up with something appropriate. And less tasty. "

I tried not to shudder, wondering what Ms. Morrigan would think was appropriate as a punishment, and less appealing than a pile of crab shells. I didn't want to find out, but I wasn't worried. I wouldn't be at all tempted to eat what

I was going to make that day. "I won't eat, Ms. Morrigan," I promised. "Not a bite."

"Get in there," she said, and shoved me toward the kitchen door. I froze, wondering if she would hear the sound of the plastic bottles in my pack, but the kitchen door swung open at that very moment and Antonio walked out, rattling two metal trays he'd carried out to clear the dishes from the tables. He bowed to Ms. Morrigan and went to work.

I went into the kitchen and opened up my backpack.

"What have you brought today, little spy?" Otto asked as he walked past my station and saw me lining up the bottles.

"Poison," I said.

That one word brought the entire kitchen to a halt.

"Have you chosen their evil?" Otto looked unbelievingly at the bottles and boxes on the counter. "Or is this something else?"

"I think poison might save us." I had to try it at least.

Vasalisa, who had been washing dishes, swung her head toward me. "What are you thinking? The witch will kill us all!"

"No," I said, trying to sound more sure than I felt. "They can't kill us all. They're getting weaker. They have to eat soon. You said it, right?"

"What of it? So they will eat the fat boy and replenish their power. It is how it has always been done." She waved a hand at the bottles. "Even if they eat the last of the bone broth today, they would taste your poison. They would know—"

"It's not poison for the witches," I said slowly. "It's poison for the students."

The staff all took a step back. One of them made the sign of the cross. Vasalisa spat on the ground and said something in her language that sounded like a curse. "What have you done? Have you joined them, then? We will not help you."

"No! It's not real poison. It's medicine." I held up one of the bottles. "I didn't have time to read through all of them, but I know some of these make people throw up. They're called emetics. Some of the others make them have to go to the bathroom," I rushed on, noticing that none of them looked any happier as I explained.

I had to get them to understand! More, I had to get them to help me. "You said they're planning to eat students starting tomorrow, right? Well, if the kids eat their food with this stuff in it, and get sick, they'll have to go home. They can't come back tomorrow. Maybe not even the next day. So, the witches will get weaker, right? Without anyone to eat, maybe they'll get weak enough that we can, I don't know . . ." I trailed off. It sounded stupid, now that I said it out loud. Stupid and impossible. What had I been thinking? Every single student would have to be out for it to work.

"Where did you get this medicine?" Otto looked more curious than angry. "There is a lot here. Enough for—"

"My stepmonster, I mean, stepmother, Molly. She wants to be super thin, but she doesn't want to stop eating chocolate, right? So she takes these to help with her 'diet.' I didn't realize she had so many until I checked this morning, though. They're not prescription, or anything."

Vasalisa's voice interrupted my thoughts. "The dose would have to be specific. Not too much, or they might die. Not too little, or they might come back tomorrow. The school lures the children. They would not want to stay home."

Otto spoke up. "The witches will suspect us. They will know we have fed them something. We will all be killed."

"Yes," Vasalisa said slowly. "We will." She looked up, fierce tears shining in her dark brown eyes. "If nothing else, we will gain freedom from this life."

"I do not want to die," Otto said. "I want to go home."

"Home?" one of the other girls said, her voice feather-soft. "I can't remember where I lived, before. I can't remember my family. Did I have a sister? A brother?"

"I remember," Antonio said. "I remember playing in the streets outside my home, the smell of my *mami*'s tortillas calling me home for lunch. I remember playing, and swimming." Others nodded.

I realized again how young the kitchen staff were. Most of them looked no older than eighteen, maybe twenty. They had all been taken by the witches when they were children themselves. Would they help me save the children she was threatening now? Kids who didn't even realize they were in trouble?

"Please," I whispered. "I can't do it alone."

Otto looked at Vasalisa.

She nodded. "We will help."

CHAPTER 23:
Poison Plan

"I still do not like it, Lorelei," Vasalisa grumbled, the same words she'd repeated for the last half hour. Lunch was only fifteen minutes away, and the trays of desserts were sitting on the warmers, ready to serve.

For all her complaints, Vasalisa had helped a lot, crumbling the bigger pills into the dough of the pastries. I'd used an old-fashioned mortar and pestle to grind up the smaller pills into a fine white dust, and added them to the powdered sugar topping on top of the marzipan.

The waiters had put the poisoned sweets on special silver platters, so they could make sure not to give any one table too much of the doctored food. We didn't want to be responsible for any kids dying or anything.

Although if a few of the mean kids like Neil Ogden ended up in the hospital, I wasn't going to send flowers.

It wasn't the poisoning that Vasalisa disapproved of, though. She didn't like the part of the plan that left me the only remaining child in a school full of hungry witches.

"It's okay," I told her again. "After lunch today, I'm going to Principal Trapp's office. I'll just tell her I'm ready to be her, um, student."

Daughter. I had almost said *daughter.*

"I won't have to pretend for long. I'll go home, and run away tonight. Once the kids are all safe, I'll be safe, too. Right?"

Vasalisa looked uncertain, but she nodded. "I hope you are right, Lorelei. I hope your idea works. These children do not deserve the death she plans."

I didn't want to think about death. I wasn't a good enough liar to fool Principal Trapp for long. But Vasalisa didn't need to know how scared I was. I heard the sounds of the first classes coming through the doors of the cafeteria, and after that, I was too busy washing dishes and plating up food to even think.

Walking past me with a tray full of tainted marzipan, Otto whispered, "Your friend Andrew is not here today. The Morrigan is very angry. You did well. He is safe."

"Thanks," I whispered back. "Is she eating broth?"

He shook his head. "There was only enough left for one. The principal has taken it. She will not be weak enough to overcome." He pulled the handle of a small paring knife out of the waistband of his black trousers. "I have this for the Morrigan. She, I may be able to fight. I will try."

Lunch ended and an hour went by in agonizing slowness. The cafeteria was quieter than it had ever been; I could hear the breathing of each worker, the frantic pounding of my heart. We finished icing the last éclair for snack—in case our plan hadn't worked—and I couldn't stand the suspense anymore. I opened the door by the playground just a crack.

A line of cars stretched around the school as parents waited to pick up their children. I watched Molly pull up and load a retching Bryan into her car. Ms. Morrigan said something to her and waved her away. Explaining that I hadn't gotten sick, I assumed.

Soon, the noise of car engines dwindled, then stopped altogether. The school was still, expectant. I was the only child left.

When the principal came into the kitchen, she was not alone. Ms. Threnody was with her. Ms. Threnody's hair looked dirty, with streaks of gray in it that made me think of stagnant water. She walked closer to me, and I smelled the unmistakable, faint hint of rotting fish. Her eyes flashed, but the lights were dim. They had been right; her magic was leaving her.

But the principal? She was as strong as ever.

"Tell me who did it," she demanded, her face fiercely beautiful. She had a stick in her hand, the wand. But the principal didn't do any magic with it; she just used it to point at the workers closest to her. "Who poisoned the children? Speak!"

No one said a word. No one breathed.

Quivering—with anger or weakness?—Ms. Threnody stepped forward and looked into Vasalisa's eyes. "Was this your idea?" she murmured, and I saw Vasalisa fight not to answer. But her eyes clouded over, just like Bryan's had in the office when she had spoken to him, and the answer came. "No."

She turned to another one of the staff. "Was it you?"

"Wait!" The principal was looking at me with a strange expression. Was she going to scream at me . . . or cry? After a few seconds, she pulled herself together and barked out, "Don't bother with them. Not a one of them has the gall to do such a thing. Ask her," she ordered, and pointed at me.

Threnody rounded on me, and the smell of dying fish

and rotting seaweed enveloped me. "You, Lorelei. Tell me." Her voice thundered like breakers on the beach. "Did you poison the children?"

"Yes," I said, not even bothering to look into her face. "I brought it from home, and put it in the desserts."

Threnody screeched and drew back her hand to hit me. But Principal Trapp said, "Stop," and everything in the kitchen froze. Her face was turned away from me, like she was afraid of what I might say. Her hair was coming down from the bun she always wore it in. It made her look tired. "Why?"

I took a deep breath. "I wanted to see if I was s-strong enough to be your d-daughter. I wanted to do something to show you I could—"

She shook her head, cutting me off. "Threnody? I'll need to borrow your gift."

Threnody nodded and slumped against the counter as the principal touched her lightly on the forehead with the wand. "Thank you. Don't be frightened. The feast will restore you, sister."

I stepped back, wondering what was going to happen, but she held up one hand. "Tell me now, Lorelei. The truth." She turned her face to me. Her eyes were brimming with tears, and my heart ached.

Even though I knew she was evil, even though I knew

she had done so many horrible things—planned to do worse—to people I loved, to children, I still remembered her hand on my hair, her smile. She had given me the love my family had taken away. She had paid attention to my pain. She had, in her own twisted way, cared for me.

"Lorelei, answer me." She stared into my face, her expression cruel.

And then, there in her eyes, I saw something I had never seen before. I saw my death.

I stopped breathing. All along, I had thought she loved me. And I had loved her. So I'd wanted to blame Ms. Morrigan, Ms. Threnody—anyone else. Even when I knew she was a witch, I had imagined that she wouldn't do anything to me. Wouldn't hurt me. I had even hoped I could change her.

What was the saying—love is stronger than anything? Even stronger than evil? My eyes burned with unshed tears. No, that wasn't it . . .

Love is blind.

It was true. I hadn't wanted to see what was right in front of me.

"What were you planning to do after you poisoned them?"

"I was planning to come to your office," I heard someone say, far away. It was me, answering.

"And what were you planning to do there?"

"I was planning to tell you I wanted to be your student," I said. "That I wanted to learn from you."

"Truly?" The whisper was hesitant, a doe sipping at a pond, a fledgling sparrow perched at the edge of its nest. "You . . . you care for me?"

The word "no" sprang to my lips, but I held it back, just barely. I reached into that raw, hungry part of my heart, that part I wished wasn't there. The part of me that had been alone, unappreciated, unloved, for so long, until she had chosen me.

Oh, if only she could have been good. I would have followed her in a heartbeat.

But she was not good. She was evil, and twisted . . . and part of me loved her anyway, because she had made *me* feel loved.

I forced the word out, pushed past the desire to tell the easy truth, and told the harder one, the deeper one instead. The truth that made no difference anyway. I was still going to have to hurt her, like I had hurt my mother. Did I care for her?

"Yes."

She leaned close and wrapped her arm around me, like I was her treasure. "I'm so glad," she whispered. "I'm so very, very glad. I didn't want you to miss tomorrow."

"Tomorrow?"

"Yes," she said. "Alva and Threnody and I have a special meal planned. One that will help us all regain our strength. We had planned on feasting this afternoon, but your little maneuver with the poison has left us with no option but to wait."

"Wait?"

"Well, of course," she said, tapping her wand against her chin thoughtfully. "The students will all be out sick. All except the one boy who stayed home. That was a stroke of luck! He'll be here tomorrow with you."

Andrew.

She paused. "Perfect. I'll let you be a part of the ceremony. You're ready for it, I think. And if you feasted with us . . . no. Too soon. And there's really only enough for three. But maybe . . . You could help us make the meal." She held me close, her fingernails running over my arms, like I was her pet. "Yes, you'll help us cook. What a day we'll have." Her nails stopped at the crook of my elbow and dug in, like she'd found a spot she wanted to pierce. "Of course, this is our little secret, you understand, sweet Lorelei. Let's keep it that way, hmm?"

"Who would I tell?" I murmured. She laughed softly, and her fingers unclenched. She had to know I wouldn't tell anyone. No one who mattered would listen anyway. We both knew there wasn't an adult in the world who would believe this story. Not like Andrew had.

I had told Andrew to stay home, and he hadn't been poisoned. The principal had enough magic left to force him into the soup pot, I was sure. He *could not* come to school tomorrow.

I had to warn him. I couldn't wait to get home, so I could do just that. Once I knew he was safe, I would run, too. I would pack my stuff and sneak out after dinner. The kitchen staff could take care of powerless witches, I hoped, as long as they didn't have any food. All I had to do was warn Andrew.

Piece of cake, right?

CHAPTER 24:
Imprisoned

I had forgotten to plan for the witch I lived with: Molly.

   She locked me in. The one night when it was honest-to-goodness life or death that I be able to get out—to call Andrew, to run away—I got home to find my stepmonster had installed a deadbolt lock on the outside of my room.

"What in the—" I started, but Molly held up one mani-cured hand.

"Not a word." She folded her arms. "I'm going to speak to your father about this, and I know he'll agree with me. This is for your own good, and the good of the family."

"What are you talking about?" I threw my backpack on the floor, and Molly's eyes widened when one of the empty medicine bottles rolled out of the half-opened zipper and onto the carpet.

"You have the nerve to question me, when the evidence is right here?" She reached down and finished unzipping the bag. She came up with three bottles in her hand. "You're sneaking out, talking on the phone to strange kids in the night? Then you're stealing medicine and taking it to school?" She stepped closer. "Every kid in the school got sick except you, Lorelei. Every kid in the school, including your own brother. Did you think I wouldn't put it together? How could you do it?"

I repeated my question, louder. "What are you talking about?"

"Don't act innocent. Your dad's been buying that act for years, but I've told him—the bad grades, the attitude, the running off. You're hanging out with a bad crowd. But I never thought you'd do something like this."

I yelled it the third time. "What are you talking about?"

She raised her hand, and for a minute I thought she was going to slap me across the face. I closed my eyes, waiting for the blow to fall, but all I heard was her angry question. "Why, Lorelei? You poisoned your classmates with my diet pills. Was it some sort of gang initiation? A bunch of those older kids I've seen in the neighborhood? You're lucky"—she grabbed my arm—"I'm not calling"—she shoved me into my room—"the police!"—and slammed the door.

I heard the lock slide into place.

"Don't even bother asking to come out, you little monster," she yelled through the door. "I'm going out. Your dad's got a late meeting, and your brother's sick as a dog, thanks to you. He's asleep. Don't wake him up."

Don't wake him up? She was the one yelling at the top of her lungs. But I didn't bother to point that out.

"What about dinner?" I yelled back instead. "Are you going to starve me to death?"

"That school of yours feeds you twice a day, Lorelei. You'll live until breakfast."

I wasn't so sure of that; I hadn't eaten breakfast or lunch. My stomach felt like it was going to cave in.

As soon as I heard her car pull out of the garage, I ran to my window. It wasn't a long drop to the ground; I would get Bryan's skateboard and . . . oh, crud. The window had been locked shut from the outside. And more than that—the lock was attached to some kind of a metal bar that went across the pane.

Wait. A metal bar?

For a minute, it didn't register. Who had done this? Dad? A handyman? Then I realized it had to have been Molly.

My own dear stepmonster had crawled up a ladder and installed a lock on the *outside* of my window.

I yanked at the window anyway. There must be some way to warn Andrew in time. Some way. My stomach growled, and I realized I needed something to eat.

Bryan was home; he would help me. "Bryan!" I yelled as loud as I could, and pounded on the wall between our rooms. "Bryan, can you hear me? I need you!" I heard moaning, so I kept pounding. "Bryan! Let me out!"

"Shut up, Lorelei," he mumbled back. "I'm sick."

"And I'm starving to death! Let me out, and I'll bring you a Sprite or something."

I heard footsteps, and then saw a dark space on the carpet at the bottom of the doorframe. "Thanks, Bryan," I said, and waited for the bolt to click open.

But it didn't. Instead, something crinkled on the floor. I leaned down. It was packets of saltine crackers. Bryan had shoved them under my door.

"Jeez, Lorelei," he muttered. "I heard Molly yelling. You poisoned us? The whole school?" A pause. "Me?"

"I had to, Bryan," I explained desperately. "I know it looks bad. But it was all I could think of."

The silence stretched into a minute, until finally, I heard him move away. "Maybe Molly's right about you."

I wanted to shove the crackers back at him, but I thought

better of it. I carried the packets to my bed and opened them carefully, sucking every last salty crumb from the wrappers before I threw them onto the rug. Then I started looking for something to break down my door.

The phone rang a thousand times—probably the neighbors asking why they kept hearing a girl screaming her head off all evening long—but no one came to my rescue. Bryan must have turned a horror flick up to full volume, because soon I heard chainsaws and screaming louder than I could manage drowning out my shouts. My voice was gone, my nails shredded from trying to pry the windows out of their frames, and my feet sore from kicking at the door.

Sobbing, I crawled onto my bed and curled my body around a pillow. I sank into despair, one thought whirling in my mind: Tomorrow, Andrew would die.

When my stomach stopped aching, I sank into sleep.

CHAPTER 25:
Running Away

"Lore-lore?" Dad opened my door quietly and sat on the edge of my bed. "You awake?"

I opened my eyes. It was early the next morning.

Dad's eyes were red-rimmed, like he'd been crying. "I'm sorry, Lore," he said. "I don't know why Molly did that. She said—she said some pretty bad things."

I'd woken in the night to the sound of their fighting. When Dad had started in on Molly about the dangers of fire hazards, accusing her of child abuse, I'd fallen back to sleep, relieved—Dad had seen it at last, figured Molly out. It was all going to be all right.

I wondered if he was going to ask about the medicines,

but he didn't. He surprised me. "I was talking to your brother a few minutes ago."

I glanced toward the door and managed a scratchy "He's okay?"

"Yes, he's fine. Stomach's still a little iffy and he's going to stay home from school today. He said"—Dad paused, and furrowed his eyebrows—"he said you've been having a hard time with your schoolwork. The writing thing." I nodded, though my schoolwork was the least of my troubles. But thank goodness Bryan was going to stay home. Hopefully the rest of the students would have to as well.

Dad wiped the back of his eyes with one hand. "I'm sorry, Lore. I should have gotten you some help before now. It's just, with your Mom, and then meeting Molly, and my work being touch-and-go . . ." He sighed. "There's no excuse. But . . . I'll get you some help, okay?"

"Okay," I rasped. He reached out to hug me. We both cried for a few minutes as he rocked me. He pulled back, and I saw his bleak expression—the expression I had put there.

"Just . . . just don't do anything dangerous, Lore. No more hurting yourself, or . . . hurting other kids. No more cries for help, okay? I heard you. I'll get you the help you need."

The help I needed? I almost laughed. He would never believe what kind of help I really needed.

He stood up abruptly and crossed to the door. "I'll get these locks off your room tonight, Lore. And we'll talk then. I have to go now. Love you."

"Dad!" I called out, but he was gone. I knew he wouldn't believe me, but I should have tried to tell him.

It was too late now. I got up and got ready for my last day of school.

Maybe my last day of anything.

Molly drove straight through the strange, wispy cloud-bank that had gathered around the school, in silence as usual. Her makeup was smeared below her eyes, like she'd forgotten to take it off the night before. She'd skipped lip-stick entirely, and her lips were gray-white and pinched, with fine wrinkles radiating out from them. She stopped the car at the crosswalk, and I peered through the fog at the school. The front doors blended into the mist like the opening to a trapdoor spider's lair. Actually, from the silence of the school and the lack of other kids or cars in the parking lot, it seemed the whole student body was safe.

Except me.

Molly let me out at the intersection, instead of at the front door, probably to get rid of me sooner, but I didn't complain. My hands were shaking so hard, I could hardly manage the door handle. Eventually, I got the door open, and Molly peeled away in a squeal of tires that echoed the internal scream I'd been suppressing.

One painful, heavy step at a time, I managed to move away from the curb. I took a deep breath as I reached the sidewalk and let my gaze wander toward the place I least wanted to be in the world. The red brick looked as cheerful as ever, the whole school as neat and normal as the first day I'd seen it. *Strange*, I thought as I walked toward the building. There were more trees today, all around the soccer fields. They hadn't been there the day before. Had they?

There was something I should remember, I thought. Something about trees. I shook the thought away. Andrew was more important than trees. *Maybe he won't come*, I thought. *Maybe he got his parents to believe him. Maybe he faked sick two days in a row. Maybe . . .*

Hope died when a blue minivan rolled past me up to the doors and let out a single passenger. Andrew.

He got out of the van and took a step toward the door.

"Andrew!" I called, but the roar of the engine must have covered the sound. The van pulled away, and I saw that Principal Trapp was there, with her hand on his arm.

I had missed my chance to warn him.

There was no way I would be able to overcome the witches. It wasn't just the magic thing; they were adults and

I was a kid. It was a matter of size. They could kill me the old-fashioned way, no spells necessary.

Even if Andrew could shake the spell, we couldn't do it, just the two of us.

The kitchen staff! I sprinted around to the side of the building, hoping no one was looking out the windows, and ran up to the side door that was closest to the cafeteria. I could see part of the playground there, and the mounds of earth beyond the climbing frames. And just past that, the soccer fields surrounded by those trees. Dozens of trees.

It didn't dawn on me, until I entered the empty kitchen, what had happened.

The copper pots sat, unwashed, in the sinks. The stove was cold, and the lights were off. They were gone. They had all disappeared. Dead?

There was something on the floor by the back door. I stepped closer and recognized it. It was the knife, the paring knife Otto had taken to kill Ms. Morrigan. Blood gleamed on the blade.

I stuffed my fist in my mouth to keep from crying out.

She never wasted anything, Otto had said.

She had changed the staff into trees.

Otto would never see his family again. Vasalisa, with her dark eyes, would stand silent guard over the bones of her sister and the mound of earth that had been her love, Gustav.

My spirit—what little courage I'd had—crumpled like a tin can underfoot. Everything was ruined; I had destroyed it with my foolish plan. I was as responsible for their deaths as I had been for my mother's.

I was the one to blame, again.

I felt dizzy and reached for the wall to steady myself.

I heard a thin, raspy laugh.

Ms. Morrigan leaned on the door, blocking my way to the cafeteria. Her hair was down and patches of it had fallen out. Her arms were covered with dark blotches that seemed to move just underneath her skin, and her face—I tried not to shudder. It was covered with oozing sores and what looked like burn marks.

She smiled, and I saw that some of her teeth were missing. The ones that were left were sharp and small, rodent-like. They were stained red, and I wondered if I was too late. Was that blood? Had she eaten Andrew? She saw me shudder, laughed again, and spoke.

"What's this? A little mouse, sneaking into the kitchen for a nibble? Are all your other mousey friends gone?" She clicked her teeth together. "What a shame. You'll have no one to play with now. Maybe I'll play with you. Hmm? Would you enjoy that?"

"N-no," I stammered. I stood up straighter. "Just . . . just leave me alone."

"Or what? You'll hurt me? Kill me?" She laughed, louder this time, then caught herself and spoke quietly. "That's what they did to poor Threnody, isn't it? The servants caught her by surprise and killed her, with a dirty kitchen knife." She smiled a small, wicked smile. "Not that I cared. Threnody never would shut up. Now it's quiet, and it's just me and my mother . . . and you, of course. We mustn't forget little gifted Lorelei."

"I'm n-not gifted," I said, taking a step back, toward the door to the playground. "You know that."

"Of course I know that, you wretched imbecile!" She glanced at the door again and then lowered her voice. I wondered who there was to hear, and then knew. The principal. She didn't know Ms. Morrigan was here, talking to me. And Ms. Morrigan didn't want her to know, either. Why not? What was going on . . . ? Then I realized. I knew the look in her eyes. I felt it every time my dad had cuddled with Molly instead of tucking me into bed, every time he had backed her up when she had been mean to me. She was jealous, jealous that Principal Trapp wanted me to be her daughter. No. More than jealous, I thought, as Ms. Morrigan stalked toward me slowly, one silent step at a time over the cold, white tile. Her eyes shone with hatred and betrayal.

"You're useless. A waste of space." She rushed toward me, and I tried to protect my face with my hands and arms.

Then I felt warm air rush past my face. Air, not her fists. I opened my eyes. She was holding the back door open.

"Go," she commanded. "Run away. Run for your life, and never come back. She has a daughter; she doesn't need a new one, a stupid one. Run away, little mouse. Go!"

My muscles bunched up to obey. I wanted to run; this was exactly what I had hoped for. It had to be a trick. What was the catch? I had to act now; I didn't have time to think.

I took a deep breath, ready to jump up—and I smelled something strange. Wood smoke. I looked away from Ms. Morrigan's face, through the doorway. I could see the playground just past her, the sand white and glimmering in the early sunlight. The trees as still as statues, not a leaf moving. There was no fire outside.

It was inside. The firewood next to the giant soup pot must have been lit. Andrew was about to be killed, and eaten, and the witches would regain their power.

"Well, mouse? What are you waiting for? Shoo." Ms. Morrigan took a step to the side, holding the door wider, and her foot rattled against something. It was the bone bucket, half-full of ground-up bone ready for the playground.

If I ran through that door, Andrew would be nothing

but soup and glimmering sand that burned blue. Of course, even if I stayed, he would probably still die.

I stood up. Ms. Morrigan smiled and laughed again; she had won.

The blood rushed out of my face. I knew I would die if I stayed.

So I ran.

CHAPTER 26:

Deeper Than Pain

I ran straight toward the door to the cafeteria, yelling the whole way.

"Principal Trapp!" I made it into the hallway before Ms. Morrigan caught me. I felt her sharpened nails cutting into my arms, her bony fingers bruising me. If the principal hadn't heard me, I was dead for sure.

But she had heard. The door to the teachers' workroom swung open, and she stepped into the hallway. She had changed. Her hair was down, falling past her shoulders in a shining black curtain. Her eyes sparked green, and her smile at seeing me disappeared when she saw Ms. Morrigan holding my arm.

"What are you doing, Alva?" she said calmly, in a voice

259

that could have frozen a lake. "Why are you hurting your little sister?"

"She's not my sister," Ms. Morrigan ground out. "My sister died last night. This little girl is nothing. She's not worthy to be one of us."

"I think you underestimate her," the principal said. "And anyway, don't forget: We need three." She flicked her fingers, and I felt Ms. Morrigan's hands fly away from my arm like I was suddenly too hot to touch. But then something strange happened. The principal wrinkled her brow in pain. Wrinkles cut deep lines into her cheeks, and around her lips. I watched her fingers move toward her pocket; she grabbed hold of something there, and it made the wrinkles disappear.

Her wand. She had her wand in her pocket.

She smiled and motioned me closer. "I think many people underestimate little Lorelei, don't they?"

I wasn't sure what she was asking, but I nodded and walked toward her. I would play along. "But not you," I said, trying for a smile.

"No, not me," she agreed. "I knew what you were capable of the first time we met. In fact, you exceeded my expectations." The side of her face twitched. "I knew you would do wonderful, terrible things; you've done them before, haven't you? But what I didn't know was how much charisma you had."

"C-charisma?"

Her eyes narrowed.

"Don't be modest," she said. "You subverted every one of my kitchen servants. You took an entire staff who had been party to years of magical conditioning to insure they never rebelled . . . and you turned them into killers in a few short days." She walked the last few steps to meet me and ran one hand over my head.

I waited for pain, but she didn't hurt me. Instead, she petted me, and I felt a warm haze of affection fill me, then fade as quickly as it had come. I glanced back at the hand that was still in her pocket; she was grasping the magic wand even tighter. She had almost no magic left, I realized. She would have to eat soon.

"Oh, Lorelei," she whispered, stroking my hair. "You will be the perfect daughter, won't you?"

"No!" Ms. Morrigan's shout echoed in the hallway, bouncing off the walls and floor. "You don't need her. We don't need her! I'm your daughter!" She rushed toward us, her shoes clapping against the floor, her hair flaring back from her withered face. "We don't need three!"

She came at me like the principal wasn't even there, came at me with her fingers stretched out toward my neck.

"You're right, Alva," Principal Trapp whispered, and

pulled the wand free from her pocket. "We don't really need three at all."

She waved her wand in the air, and static electricity rushed over my skin.

The magic came and went, leaving Ms. Morrigan on the floor, a pile of bones that turned to dust as we watched. The dust wasn't white. It was black and gray, flecked with silver. It wouldn't make good playground sand, I thought, trying not to laugh hysterically.

The principal turned to me, and the emotion on her face faded slowly, replaced by a flat expression that had no spark, no soul behind it. "Now for you."

My breath started coming faster, like I was running a race, though I was standing still. I could feel my pulse pound in my temples, in my neck, in my ears. I heard someone panting, fast, too fast. In seconds, there were stars blinking at the corners of my eyes.

"Breathe deeply, dear," the principal said. "You're hyperventilating. I can't have you passing out now, can I? I'm going to need your help." I tried to breathe slowly, and she kneeled down next to me, staring into my eyes. I swam in those deep, green pools for a moment or two, long enough to remember how to breathe, how to think. Her eyes shone with tears—for Alva? She had killed her own daughter. She *should* cry.

"You killed your daughter," I said, without thinking. "How?"

Green eyes flared with cold fire. "As easily as you killed your mother, Lorelei."

"Not like that," I said. "It wasn't like what you did." My eyes moved back to the pile of gray dust. How had she done it? Destroyed someone she had loved for years, decades maybe, without blinking. Now, *that* was evil.

Inside, something began to move, the solid weight that had pressed against my heart shifting after a year of pain. It moved slowly, like the earth when a seed underneath finally sprouts and pushes upward. Something was unfurling in my mind, a new idea, growing.

I had never done anything like that. I couldn't have.

"It was exactly like that," she murmured. "Minus the wand, I'm sure. But death is death. Murder is murder."

"I never said I *murdered* my mother." The idea grew a bit more, a soft shoot showing through the hard-packed earth.

Her fingers were cold on my face, as cold as Ms. Morrigan's had ever been.

"That's the thing about being with me. You didn't have to say it out loud"—she paused to run her hand down my long hair—"silly little Lorelei bird."

Threnody had called me that, too, I remembered. Right before she had forced me to sing. She had been trying to make fun of the way my mother had sung to me. Now Principal Trapp was doing the same thing.

More jealousy. The principal was jealous of the love I felt—still felt—for my mother.

Principal Trapp had said she had a dark secret, too. She wanted someone who knew this, loved her anyway, and accepted her. She wanted me to be as evil as she was, needed to believe I was like her. Why?

She was lonely like me. No one else understood. No one else had done what she did. No one else had killed her own mother.

I looked again at the pile of dust that had been Ms. Morrigan.

The thought blossomed at last. If this was killing, I hadn't killed Mom.

I hadn't looked into my mother's eyes and wished her death. So maybe . . . just maybe. I thought of Mom, of the way she had looked on that terrible day, and in the hospital. I remembered, and waited for the pain.

But the pain never came. The dried splinters of guilt that had pressed against me for so long were fading, changing into something else, something tender and familiar. I took a deep breath, and for a moment, smelled the skin on my mother's neck.

The memory made me smile.

"What is that smile? What have you done?" the principal murmured. Our eyes were still locked. "You were dark inside, as dark as me, a moment ago. And now . . ." She began to tremble, like a volcano threatening to erupt. "There's not a shadow of evil on your useless heart. What have you done?"

"I woke up," I said, wondering at the lightness inside me. I took another breath, and for the first time in more than a year, the bands of pain that had been on my heart were gone. As I breathed, memories of my mother flashed through my mind, brushing petal-soft against my heart as they appeared. Her quick smile, her voice, light and meadowlark high, her eyes that were—now that I could hold the memory of them in my mind without the familiar agony of guilt—not at all the same green as the principal's. The memories of my mother filled me until I had to fight not to shout from the sheer joy of holding her in my mind again. "You were wrong. I didn't kill my mother."

"I looked into your mind. You remembered it," she shouted. "You were certain of it!"

"Then I was wrong, too. I loved my mother. And I love my father and even Bryan, too. They're my family." I remembered the words my dad had said when he dropped me off at Splendid that first day. "Family takes care of family."

"You have nothing in common with those people, Lorelei. You're like me." Her voice was pleading now, lonely. I supposed she was alone. All of her servants changed into trees and hills, Threnody gone, her adopted daughter dead by her own hand. "Some of us have to make our own families, sweetheart. I chose you. I *chose* you."

A tear fell down her face and splashed onto her white blouse.

I heard a muffled sound from the back of the workroom. It sounded like panting and a smothered gasp of pain.

Andrew.

I spoke up. "I know you chose me. But I can't—I

won't—choose you. Your life. I don't want to hurt anyone else."

Another tear fell. "Don't you care that you're hurting me?"

I thought about Vasalisa and Gustav. About Otto. The truth was hard, but I spoke softly.

"No."

She straightened an inch at a time, her eyes growing wintry as she pulled away. "Stupid little girl. Alva was right about you. Alva . . ." Her voice trailed off, as she looked back at the remains of her daughter, now a mound of dark sand and fabric scraps on the floor. "You'll pay for that."

The wand appeared in her hand. "Into the room. You'll help with the feast, and then . . . I'll show you what it means to be my family. Everything you can be, what you can do. You'll change your mind."

"I won't," I said, looking away.

"Maybe. Maybe not. Maybe I'll just have to console myself," she said, her voice filled with bitter laughter. "Waste not, want not, isn't that right?" I turned my head back. She was licking her lips, watching me like a cat watches a sparrow. "Scrappy, aren't you? I'll have to watch for bones."

She jabbed me forward with her wand into the workroom. Andrew was tied up with very non-magical-looking rope in the corner, and the enormous copper soup pot was sitting across the room on a giant, flat metal base that looked like steel. Wood had been stacked all around the bottom of the pot and was burning merrily, crackling and popping like it could hardly wait for the feast. The window was open, and the smoke from the burning wood poured out through the small opening, but the smell filled the room.

The witch shoved me into the room and pulled the door shut behind us. The lock clicked and her wand was in her hand again.

"Pile more logs under the pot," she ordered, and I found myself moving toward the pile of wood by the wall, even though I didn't want to.

Was she still that powerful? I looked back. Her hair was mussed; she ran her fingers through it, patting it back, and I saw a clump of it come away in her hand. "Bah!" she muttered, and threw the hair into the fire. It smelled like burning rubber. The smoke that poured out seared my nostrils.

She was getting weaker. Maybe I could stop walking. I resisted the urge to run to the woodpile and found I could move smoothly, slowly. I could—almost—stop altogether.

I picked up the firewood and set it down, just far enough from the fire that it couldn't possibly light, and shuffled back, slowly, to get the second load.

"What are you doing?" The witch's voice was shrill for the first time.

"What do you mean?" I asked, stalling for time. "I put the logs under the pot."

"Closer to the fire, you stupid girl," she rasped. "Right into the flames."

"Oh," I said, nodding like I'd just understood. "This way?" I picked up one of the logs and threw it at the burning wood. Sparks flew. Just as I'd hoped, the log jostled the other pieces of wood away from the pot. The water in the pot would never boil at this rate. I could do this all day.

"No, you idiot," she yelled, and pointed her wand at me. "Fix it."

I felt my body jerk under her spell, and I reached for the logs that had scattered—reached with my bare hands, grabbing the smoldering embers, unable to stop—and shoved them back into the flames.

My hands seared. I staggered from the pain, screaming, and found my mouth shut by the witch's magic. The room was silent—and then I heard a sound over my own silent agony.

It was Andrew. He was crying, tears running down his face, his whimpers growing louder. His eyes said everything his mouth couldn't. I saw pride, and pain, and affection in them.

I pushed my thoughts away from my hands. I could ignore them. I had to. The witch was almost weak enough.

"Now, girl," I heard through the haze of pain, "come and"—a harsh giggle—"check the water for me."

I just stood there. What did she mean, check the water? The pot was huge—I couldn't reach that high. She must have seen the question on my face, since she released my mouth to speak. But as soon as I could speak, the pain returned. I howled my throat raw in seconds.

"Stop that noise," she commanded, and waved her wand again. I watched her face grow wrinkled and smaller as she did it, but the pain vanished completely. I looked down; my hands were whole again. She had healed them. Why?

"Are you really that stupid?" she said. "Check the water!"

I looked around and saw a small, golden stepstool next to the pot. The metal on the step was carved with dozens of unicorns, running, jumping, rearing. I reached down and touched it. It felt like real gold, soft as the copper pot, warm from the fire. I used it to shove a few logs away from the side of the pot and climbed up, taking the first step carefully.

I tested one finger against the side of the copper pot and yanked it away. It was blisteringly hot, and I inched closer, cautious. Warm moist air rushed past me, and I stared into the pot. There was nothing there but bubbling water. No vegetables, no meat, no rice. Just water. Water that would cover my head, I realized. I couldn't see the bottom. If I fell—if anyone fell into that pot, they would never be able to climb out, not before they were cooked.

"Test it," Principal Trapp cackled behind me. Her voice was filled with joy. "Go ahead, test it. Is it hot enough?" I saw her, out of the corner of my eye, moving toward me. Her hands were stretched out, ready to hold me there . . . or push me in.

Quickly, I stepped down off the stool. "How?" I asked, looking up at her like she had switched to Portuguese.

"What do you mean, how?" The witch looked confused for a moment, then angry. "How stupid are you, you little brat?"

How stupid was I? I was about to find out. "I don't have a spoon, or anything. I'm not a cook; you know I'm just a kid. I never boiled water before in my life." I stared into her angry face, reaching inside for the expression I needed to convince her I was really *trying*—but I couldn't.

Of course, thanks to years of not being able to write reports and essays—semester after semester of getting Allison or one of my other friends to help write the answers that I knew but couldn't put on paper—I knew exactly how that felt. I poured every ounce of my frustration into my voice.

"I would do it," I said, and sniffled, "if I knew how."

"How could I have been so wrong about you?" Principal Trapp asked herself, and stepped up on the stool. "I'll show you, stupid. First you step on the stool," she slowed her voice down, and pitched it higher, like she was talking to a baby. The way Bryan did when he wanted to make fun of me. "Then you lean over, and stretch your hand out"—I stepped up on the stool behind her, holding my breath— "and you put your hand into the water to see if it's—"

"Hot enough?" I finished for her as I shoved her into the boiling pot, head first.

Her foot kicked out as she slipped past me, knocking me to one side. I fell off the stool just in time. The soup pot exploded with black smoke, great pillars of smoke that curled around themselves like hands clawing at one another. A sound came from inside the pot, a high-pitched squealing like a rabbit being killed. And then the smoke was gone, racing out the window, carrying the hideous smell with it, leaving me alone.

No, not alone.

I raced over to Andrew's side, knelt down, and began to work at the ropes. "Andrew, are you okay? She didn't hurt you, did she?" The ropes were slippery. I couldn't untie any of the knots. As soon as I untangled one, the rope itself would snarl into a larger knot a few inches away.

"Ugh," I said. It felt like snakes in my hands, and Andrew was only tied tighter. "I thought . . . you know, she's dead, right? I thought the magic would be gone."

Andrew made a muffled noise, and I saw his eyes dart to a spot right behind me.

Oh, no. I knew what this meant. I had seen this moment in a hundred scary movies, yelled, "You idiot!" at dozens of girls who had turned their back on the bad guy, thinking he was gone, only to have him come at them from behind.

She wasn't dead.

Before I turned, I felt her, her breath on my neck, her eyes burning me, her hands on my skin. I had never been so frightened in my life. I turned anyway.

CHAPTER 27:

Set Free

No one was there. It had been my imagination. But, wait—there was something. On the ground, right behind me. A small stick—a whittled tree branch—nothing to be scared of at all. I picked it up.

Her wand. But now, of course, there was no witch to use it. Unless . . .

Was I like her? Really? Even if I hadn't killed my mother, I *had* killed the principal, or made her turn into smoke anyway. I was a murderer, or close enough, and I didn't even feel bad about it.

Deep down, maybe she had been right. Maybe I was witch material. I held the wand out, pointed it at Andrew, and willed the rope to untie.

It fell away in gleaming, silver coils, like a pet, a snake that did tricks for me.

"L-Lorelei?" Andrew stood up, slowly, like an old man. "Are you . . . you are Lorelei, right?"

"What do you mean?" I asked. My voice sounded different—strong, confident. Smooth. I looked at the side of the copper kettle; it gleamed, reflecting me.

But a different me. I had black curls now, a gorgeous, long curtain of hair. I stared at the wand. Did magic change you? Was the wand helping me . . . or making me into something else?

Whatever it was, it felt good, right. I felt strong. I could run a hundred miles, climb a hundred trees.

Trees! I remembered the trees. The kitchen staff. "Come with me," I shouted to Andrew, and raced for the door. He limped along behind me. I held the door open for him, impatient, and had to keep myself from pushing him through it. I felt like, if I waited, they would be gone. Like the school, the property around us, and everything on it could disappear in a blink.

"There they are," I whispered. The trees were bowing in the sudden wind that swept across the field. I ran to them, hearing the voices of my friends in their rustling leaves. I stopped, and held the wand up, willing it to change them.

But the voices cried out. *No*, they rustled, and more insistently—*you must not!*

Why not? I thought back at them. There was no answer, and I raised the wand again. The wind shrieked around my hair, and I saw it flying, black as a raven's wing, dark and beautiful and strange, around my shoulders.

You will become one of them, the leaves answered in the wind. *You are changing now.*

It was true. I knew it.

The branches of the close-rooted trees rubbed together, like arms holding each other up. *Friendship*, they seemed to say, in the soft scrape of bark against bark. *Love. Family.*

"What do I do?" I whispered. "I want to save you, too. I *can* save you. You don't have to . . . die."

The leaves began to fall, great green flakes swirling around my head. *We are already dying*, they said as they fell. *You cannot save us.*

You can only set us free.

I looked at the branch in my hand. I thought I knew what I needed to do. But if I was wrong . . .

Set us all free.

Something peppered the back of my neck and my hair, and I turned. It was sand from the playground, blowing away. Great clouds of white, glittering dust swept around the field and into the sky, becoming transparent, shifting as they rose. All those children, magical again. The sand vanished into the sky, and I knew they were going home at last. They were free.

A leaf caught in my hair, and I heard Vasalisa's whisper. *Set yourself free, Lorelei. You know how. Clever, clever girl.*

I heard her laughter in the wind, and I knew what to do.

I broke the wand over my knee, splintering it into two ragged twigs.

It was over.

CHAPTER 28:
Finally Forgiven

ndrew and I sat on the edge of the drainage ditch full of water. The field behind us was flat. No mounds of earth, no trees. The school itself looked like it was twenty years old and the playground equipment looked older, rusted, and warped. As I watched, one of the seesaws cracked into two pieces and fell with a soft thunk onto the raw earth below.

"Are you okay?" Andrew asked, reaching for my hands. He lifted one of them up. "You're scratched. Bleeding, a little."

Surprised, I looked down. I hadn't felt anything. But there, across both palms, were marks. It looked like I had been beaten with a thin branch.

I shifted, feeling the broken pieces of the wand—now

just a handful of splintered wood—move in my back pocket. I hadn't wanted to leave the pieces on the ground; broken or not, it seemed like a bad idea to throw them away. "Could have been worse," I said. "How are you?"

"Good as new," Andrew said. "Hungry, though." We both laughed. "What happened, Lorelei? Where are the other kids? Did she—"

"No," I interrupted. "They're all fine. Well, puking up their guts, but they'll live." I told him about the medicine, and the kitchen staff, and Molly locking me in so I couldn't warn him. "I'm sorry," I said.

"Are you kidding?" His eyes were saucer-big. "You came back to save me! That's the bravest thing I've ever heard." He leaned back, looking like a startled hedgehog with his dark hair poking up worse than ever. "I can't believe it!" A pause. "You know, no one else will believe it either."

"I know. And no one would listen to us anyway. They're grown-ups. They'll come up with some explanation for it. They always do."

Andrew cleared his throat. "You still have a streak of black in your hair, you know."

I pulled a piece toward me. "Huh. Yeah, I do. Oh, well. They'll just think I dyed it."

"What are you going to do now?" Andrew asked, standing up.

I stood up next to him and looked down into the drain-age ditch. It was slowly emptying out, the salt water that had filled it the night before trickling away, downhill. "I'll go home. Eat, sleep. Come back here when this ditch is empty and see if I can salvage Bryan's skateboard."

"Will you teach me to skate?" he asked. "If you think someone like me could do that." He looked down, his cheeks turning pink. I got it. He thought he was too fat. I tilted my head to look at him. He would actually look really good in skater clothes. Baggy jeans, a chain or two.

"Well, I would," I said, "if I knew how. I'm awful at it. Haven't you seen my knees?" We both laughed. "How about I ask Bryan if he'll teach us both?"

"That sounds fun," Andrew said, smiling at the ground. He shuffled his feet back and forth for a few seconds, like he was thinking about something. Then, still looking at the ground, he asked a question. "You know how the principal said you murdered your mother? You never really thought that, did you?"

I had completely forgotten Andrew had been in the room for that conversation. "Yeah, I did," I said. "I really did think that."

It felt strange not to hurt; I had been in pain so long the pain itself had become something real. And now it was gone. It reminded me of losing a tooth, when you can still remember what it felt like, but you can't feel it anymore, the hole where it had been the only thing left.

"Wow," Andrew said. "I didn't know you felt that way. You always seemed so . . . strong, I guess."

"Me, strong?"

"You forgave yourself. That takes a lot of strength, Lorelei." He shrugged. "At least, that's what my therapist tells me."

I almost laughed. He was right! I'd gotten rid of a witch, saved the lives of hundreds of kids. But only Andrew could understand I'd done something even harder. I'd forgiven myself. I'd set the memory of my mother free. I could almost hear her voice, singing to me in the breeze that blew past. I held one stinging palm up to my ear, and for a few seconds, I *did* hear her voice.

Magic? Or just memory?

"Thanks, Andrew," I said after a few seconds. "I guess I was strong enough at the end."

The silence between us stretched out, both of us thinking of the principal's last few moments, until Andrew nudged the dirt with the toe of one of his sneakers. "So . . . skateboarding with Bryan, huh?"

"Definitely," I answered. "Saturday work for you?"

"Yeah," he said. "I'll walk you home. We can make up our alibis on the way."

"Thanks. I'm not looking forward to telling Molly I boiled the principal up in a giant soup pot."

Andrew stared, like he couldn't believe what I'd said . . . and then, his lips wiggled. Twitched. Jerked up and down, and up again, like he wasn't sure whether to frown disapprovingly or laugh. I smiled. He snorted. Within seconds, we had to hold each other up, we were laughing so hard— not from humor, but from sheer relief, and the knowledge that no one would ever believe what we had to say.

My hands itched and I peered at them. Something was still there. I could just make out three tiny splinters of wood in each of my palms, buried deep under the skin. I flexed my fingers, and six droplets of blood welled up by the splinters, each droplet as round and red as a pomegranate seed. Six reminders of everything that had changed.

I thought of Persephone, going home to her mother after six months with Hades. I was going home, sure, but my mother was the one who would never return. At least I had the memory of her now, I thought. Without the old, sharp guilt pressing into me, I could love my mother, love her memory, as much as I wanted to. I knew this was what she would have wished for me.

I was strong. I could live with a few splinters of wood

in my hands, even if they did burn. Now that I'd healed my heart? I could have a thousand real splinters and never stop singing.

The feeling of the splinters faded when I walked, changing as I moved away from the school. My world was still changing, all around me, I thought. But now, I had a feeling I was the one making the changes. Could I make the one that was most important and figure out how to fix my family?

I'd gotten rid of three witches already. Rehabilitating one wicked stepmother couldn't be that hard. For all I knew, Molly was as lonely as Principal Trapp had been. As I had been.

It was worth a try.

I could always toss her in a soup pot if she wouldn't stop being such a witch.

Acknowledgments

If not for the inimitable and fearless Suzie Townsend, I would never have had the courage to write this book. Suzie, you are truly splendid. Thank you as well to Laura Arnold for her sure guidance and vision, and for saying yes!

Sweet thanks to friends and first readers: Lindsey Scheibe, Sam Bond, Lori Walker, Laura Jennings, Pamela Hutchins, Holly Green, Tricia Mathison, and Sheryl Witschorke.

A chocolate-covered thank you to my critique partner and dear friend, Shelli Cornelison. They will, indeed, rue the day.

To Cynthia, Debbie, Bethany, and all the Awesome Austin Writers, for their invaluable support through the whole process—you really are awesome.

Family takes care of one another, and reads manuscripts, too. Lari, Rae, Taryn, Cameron, Drew, Dave, and the entire Borg: I love y'all.

I want to recognize the excellent teachers who allowed me to read countless books under my desk while I was supposed to be doing schoolwork, and the librarians who gleefully provided them. You won't find yourselves in this story—but you are in my heart forever.

Continue reading for a peek at another magical tale
by Nikki Loftin. . . .

"This is a work of tremendous heart."
—Anne Ursu, author of Breadcrumbs

Nightingale's
Nest

Nikki Loftin

Chapter 1

When I first heard Gayle, I couldn't tell if she was a bird or a girl. All I knew for sure was that the music she made wasn't like anything I'd heard before. It was magic.

Even a kid like me could recognize that.

I'd just come from clearing brush on the Emperor's property. He wasn't really an emperor, of course. His name was Mr. Azariah King, but he'd owned a chain of those almost-everything-for-a-dollar stores in our part of Texas for years, called Emperor's Emporiums, so everybody called him the Emperor.

Except for my dad. He hated the man. But not enough to turn down a steady ten-week job for the summer, even if it was almost a hundred degrees most days. Money was money, and our landlord wasn't going to wait until a better job came along, Mom told us. Dad said he wasn't as worried about rent as he was about getting our cable TV hooked up again; he hadn't been able to catch a single baseball game since the end of May.

So Dad, the Big John of Big John's Tree and Brush Removal, had taken the job to work on the Emperor's failing pecan trees, all 104 acres of them. As for me, I was only twelve, but I'd grown seven inches in nine months. Dad said I was old enough and strong enough to learn how to work with trees during summer vacation. And if I messed up, cut too deep into one of the Emperor's pecans and killed it? He said that would serve the money-grubber right.

I didn't care if I killed a tree, either. I thought the world would be a better place if every tree in it was cut down.

The first thing I noticed that day was the birds. They had flown away, like they usually did, at the sound of Dad's chain saw. But I saw that they had all flown in the same direction, and kept going over the Emperor's tall wooden fence to the neighboring property. That property belonged to Mrs. Cutlin, a widowed lady with one jerk of a son about my age, although they always had some other kids hanging around—she fostered orphans. Not because she was the kind of person who cared about kids, or at least I didn't think so. Dad and I had heard her yelling at her son for the past few weeks. When I'd asked Dad about it, he'd said, "Fostering a kid's worth six hundred dollars a month. Whole town knows she needs the money."

Anyway, there was a tree there, a tall sycamore that grew close to the Emperor's fence line, close enough that some of the branches reached over. I was hauling cut limbs to a place that looked about right for a burn pile, and that's when I saw where the birds had gone.

They were perched in the sycamore, hundreds of them. It looked like someone had taken a paintbrush to the thing, what with all the reds and blues—cardinals and scrub jays—in between the wide leaves. Dozens of sparrows sat along the lower branches, mixed in with black-capped chickadees, finches, wrens, and flycatchers. I even counted four painted buntings, with their rainbow coats, before I realized what was wrong.

None of the birds were singing. They weren't making a single sound.

But something was. Or someone.

I'd never heard a song like it before. I couldn't imagine anyone in the world had.

The notes were high and liquid, a honey-soft river of sound that seeped right through me. I stopped when I heard the first notes and just stood there, dropping cedar cuttings at my feet.

The song sailed over the fence, like it was meant for me alone. No words to it. It was pure melody. I felt almost like my feet were lifting away from the ground, that the only thing holding me to earth was my own belief in gravity.

The song went on, and I peered through my watering eyes at the branches. There was something there. Something bigger than a bird. A collection of stacked twigs and branches, bits of twine, and what seemed to be wire wrapped around it all, holding it together. A nest, it looked like. And the sound was coming from inside.

I took a step toward it, and my foot hit a twig.

The birds heard me first, and they all took flight, enormous confetti swirling into the sky.

Then the music stopped, and I felt my heart constrict, like I'd lost something precious.

I took another step, and another, until I could see through the leaves. That's when I realized the singer was a person. A little girl. She was plain, with brown hair the same color as mine. But hers was ratted around her face like she'd never seen a brush, and she had dirt smeared across her cheeks and nose. *Too thin*, I thought, as she climbed over the edge of the bundled mess of sticks and out onto a branch to see me better. She was awfully close to the slender branches that I knew wouldn't hold the weight of a kid, even a skinny little girl.

I had to get her to come down before she hurt herself. But she looked as frightened of me as the birds had been. As if she might fly away like they had, if I spoke too suddenly.

First, I'd have to get her to trust me.

"Who are you?" I asked in my softest voice. "Was that you singing?" As she inched closer, I realized she must be about eight years old.

The same age my sister, Raelynn, had been.

My heart constricted a bit more. "That was you, right?"

She nodded, her head bobbling like a heavy sunflower on a too-narrow stalk, and edged out a bit more on the branch. Her feet were bare, and dirty. Her toes were as thin as the rest of her, and kind of long—she used them to clutch the branch she was on just like a baby bird would.

"It was beautiful," I said, almost whispered. "The most beautiful thing I ever heard."

She blushed a little.

"What's your name?"

She didn't answer. She looked confused, like she wasn't certain what I'd asked.

Maybe she didn't speak English, I thought. Or maybe she was touched, like my grandma used to say when she meant *crazy.* I tried again: "You got a name?"

"Gayle," she said, clearing her throat to repeat the word. Her speaking voice was unsteady, like she wasn't used to talking. "I'm Gayle."

I recognized the roughness of too many tears cried in the sound of her words. It was the same way my own voice had been for a long time.

Something had happened to her, something bad.

I spoke a little louder and tried to smile. "I'm Little John." I lifted my arms, flexed the muscles, and made a constipated/mad face like one of the Wrestling Federation guys on TV. I knew it made me look ridiculous, lips pulled back from my teeth, my eyes crossed. But I wanted her to laugh at me. "Little, on account of I'm so small and puny."

Laughter spilled down for a split second. "You're not little."

"Sure I am," I said. "It just looks like I'm big from up there. It's a—what do you call it?—an optical illusion. Why don't you come and see for yourself? Climb on down. Careful, though. That rotten tree isn't sturdy enough for an *enormous* girl like you."

The laughter pealed out again, and I saw her reach out to the tree trunk and hug it, of all things. "It's okay," she whispered to the trunk. "You're not rotten." Like it was her friend, and I'd hurt its feelings. Her feet looked unsteady on the high branch, and the leaves all around her were shaking.

I had to get her down. "Stop fooling around," I tried again, wiping away the sweat that was running into my eyes. "It's not safe up there. You're too high." I had an idea. "I'll get you a piece of candy if you come down. Just do it now, all right?"

She had to come down. If she waited any longer, I was going to have a heart attack.

"Okay," she said. But then she didn't move. She just started humming under her breath, the same tune she'd been singing, but softer this time. It still brought tears to my eyes.

At least I thought that's what was happening. It must have been, because as I watched her, and listened to the music, the singing that got louder and louder, clearer and higher and purer, she got . . . fuzzy around the edges. *Her outline was against the sun,* I thought. That's why she seemed to blur. It was awful hot; maybe it was just the flickering mirage of heat lines.

I wiped my eyes again and squinted up at her. The more she sang, the more she seemed to shimmer against the sky, her edges feathering into the background blue.

Her voice was loud now, so loud I couldn't have stopped the sound even by plugging my ears. Through the melody, though, I heard something squeal and slam behind me, on the other side of the fence. A door.

Someone else was listening.

I turned and saw the Emperor, a hundred yards back, standing outside his back door, a deep purple velvety robe flapping around his bony legs. He was staring at the tree, mouth wide open, watching the girl. The sunlight glinted on his wrinkled, wet cheeks. I wondered, for a moment, at the sight of a grown man crying. But her voice . . . it was the kind that could bring anyone to tears, I figured.

Cra-ack! I knew the sound of a branch cracking. I whirled back around.

That's when I realized the girl had to be touched. She hadn't started to come down at all—she'd started to climb out on the branch, toward me. She was perching, hopping like a wren, further and further out on one of the limbs that wouldn't hold her.

I knew what was going to happen next. She was going to go out too far on the branch, and it would snap under her. She would fall, screaming, in a shower of small branches, leaves, and bark.

It was the nightmare I had every night.

I wouldn't be there to catch her. I never made it to the base of the tree in time, my legs too small, too short, my hands reaching out at the ends of arms too weak to hold her anyway.

And I would have to watch her snap like a bough herself, on the ground, the blood as red as a cardinal's wing.

It was the nightmare I'd lived once before.

And the reason I had devoted my life to cutting down every tree in the world.

Every last murderous tree.

The girl screamed as she fell, and I raced to catch her, knowing I would be too late.